from Tangled Roots

TODD R. GUNDERSON

Hildebrand Books
an imprint of W. Brand Publishing

NASHVILLE, TENNESSEE

Hildebrand Books is an imprint of W. Brand Publishing.
j.brand@wbrandpub.com
www.wbrandpub.com

Printed and bound in the United States of America.

Cover design by designchik.net
Cover Illustration by Ellen Hokanson

From Tangled Roots / Todd R. Gunderson–1st edition

Paperback ISBN 978-1-950385-45-4
eBook ISBN: 978-1-950385-46-1
Kindle

Library of Congress Number: 2020947145

Contents

Dedicated to my wonderful parents, Howard and Evelyn,
who instilled in me the courage to go my own way,
the steadfastness to continue my way, and the sound
Christian wisdom that lights my way.

CHAPTER 1

Seventeen

The cars arrived one by one, some parking in the street, others in the yard. The only car allowed in the driveway was Carrie's. It had a large red bow atop, and cards taped to its windows. The used Toyota Corolla was in great shape. The silver color shone in the sunlight. The special chromed window louvers glistened, too, as if kissed by the sun. With all the festivities about to take place, Carrie sat alone on the porch swing, contemplating where the time had gone. The youth she once knew had mysteriously disappeared, and the carefree spirit of her past was changing into a new chapter—quite unwelcomed. Responsibility would be the new buzz word as she would be expected to raise money for the endless bills that accompanied car ownership. Despite this, she reassured herself that her seventeenth birthday would also bring new freedoms, but they would come at a cost. The mind games she played, and the self-derogating would have to wait as she heard several people call out her name.

"Carrie, it's time! Come on, sweetheart!" called her mother.

"Coming, Mom!" she hollered back, but just before she caught a glimpse of her Uncle Wit. She knew what was coming before he opened his mouth to say it, a hardy, "Wha'cha gonna do with your life there, girl?"

He had asked her that last week at a Labor Day family reunion, and it was one reason she was a little distraught on the day of her birthday. The girls at school were all talking about their futures, their plans, their likes and dislikes, their loves and even marriage, but Carrie could not come to a conclusion about any of it. She didn't want to be thinking about it. She was only seventeen. There was plenty of time for that, or was there? Not in the eyes of so many, as graduation loomed ahead, there seemed to be a negative connotation on her indifference about the future. She had heard this question so many times in the past month she thought she would scream if she heard it again. Her friends were all ahead of her in age due to her birthdate; she started school much younger. Her melancholy at this juncture could be traced to a bit of apprehension in taking the necessary life steps; it was her maturity level, but she didn't like to think of it in those terms—inexperience was her word.

"Uncle Wit, do you have to ask me that today of all days? I told you last week that I had no idea." They were slowly walking to the backyard where the party would get started. She was not rude, but she rolled her eyes enough for Uncle Wit to take the clue.

"I know, I know," he said. "I just don't want you to blow in the wind forever like I did. I took a leave of absence from my wits when I was young. Maybe that's why they call me Wit." He laughed.

Carrie didn't find it too amusing but laughed to help engage herself for what was around the corner. The backyard was transformed into a carnival of sorts. Balloon bouquets and streamers of all colors were hanging from trees and posts. A large cake centered the backyard on a round table borrowed from the living room.

"Mom! Where did you get all this stuff? I'm glad I stayed in the front; what a surprise!" She laughed.

Her grandmother was standing by the cake and stared at her with dreamy eyes. It seemed she was remembering herself at seventeen. The large cake server in her hand was shaking back and forth from her mild Parkinson's disease, but the smile on her face was so proud. There were so many people there, and Carrie stared in disbelief at the benevolence of so many. The gifts were piled up under the round table. A large smile filled Carrie's face. It was a smile that was true and happy; the troubles she was previously pondering left her in an instant as thunderous applause was offered.

"Happy Birthday!" they all cried.

"I don't know what to say." Carrie shuffled her feet in shyness. "Thank you all for this; I can't believe it. Look at all those presents!"

Her parents, Allen and Carla, were not wealthy, yet the party seemed fit for a queen. Her parents were popular in town; they both ran an animal relocation and euthanasia clinic for wild and domestic animals. The money was not the best, but it paid the bills. Often, they gave all they had to help the homeless animals abandoned or found injured on the side of the road; the interstate travel nearby necessitated the clinic. Carrie figured money would be short this month for sure by the looks of things; not to mention the car in the front drive.

"So, you do like it?" Her mother didn't wait for a response. "We knew you would, sweetheart," her mother cried. Carrie was nodding her head vigorously, and she felt like a little girl on Christmas morning.

"Mom, Dad, thank you so much. Thank you all." She blushed again. "Wow, I just don't know what to say."

"Speech! Speech!" one voice called out. "We want to hear a speech from the pretty seventeen-year-old."

Carrie lifted her hands in self-defense. "I can't. I don't see any pretty seventeen-year-olds around here, and I don't know what to say."

Carrie latched on to the word pretty. She didn't feel pretty. She thought she was. . .okay, perhaps, but not pretty. Before she took it too far, she remembered her mother's little speech about rudeness, walked over to the table with the cake, and began to preach. *Pretty or not,* she thought, *I'll get my point across.*

"Okay, okay," she pleaded. "Thank you all so much. I just want to say that you will all probably get sick of me driving over to your houses now that I have a car. I might even ask for gas money, too." Several laughed at her joke. "But, whatever you do, don't ask me what I'm going to do with my life, because I have no clue. So, if anyone has any good ideas, I'm listening. I just want to make a lot of money, so give me the good ideas first." She laughed. "Now let's eat!"

"Carrie!" her mother called in a high tone. "You can't say that; don't you have something else to say?"

But it was too late, thirty-some guests rushed the table for cake and laughs with Carrie. She had no lingering sadness at this time. It wasn't long after the speech that several of the guests questioned her while she was eating. She quickly realized that the speech was not the smartest thing she could've said. Now everybody recognized her problem. *Inexperience,* she thought. "I wish I had thought that one through," she said out loud to her mother as she sat down.

"You'll just have to listen to the advice; you don't have to use it, but at least listen," her mother said quietly as she sat down next to her.

"You don't have any plans?" her grandmother asked.

"I didn't know you were on the fence about your future," said a neighbor.

"You can come work for me," Mr. James said. "I could always use another pizza delivery girl."

"I heard glamour school is popular with girls these days, especially if you're not sure what you want to do. I've been thinking about it; we could go together," her good friend Teresa comforted.

Carrie smiled more during the evening than she had the whole year. She was thankful that so many people were trying to help, but the input was all too much for her to consider at the time. In a way, it only depressed her more.

Uncle Wit watched Carrie's interactions with her friends and neighbors. The look on his face was of worry, and he paced back and forth across the backyard near the fence all evening. Carrie's mother left her side and confronted him.

"You're acting kinda funny," she told him. "You're going to kill the grass if you don't stop."

"It's my fault Carrie said that stuff today," he told her mother. "I was bothering her earlier in the week about it at the reunion. I can tell it's weighing heavily on her. I want to help her so badly, but I don't know how. I only wanted her to think about the future."

"Oh, so you're the one; I knew somebody had said something to her based on the way she was acting this week. Ya know, it's just like the way you ran me into the ground while growing up. I get it now, it makes more sense to me, thanks for sharing," Carrie's mother said angrily.

"Aw, come now, it shouldn't bother her that much, should it?" he questioned.

"Do you have any idea what a teenage girl goes through these days? You sure didn't when I was growing up. There's a lot of pressure on these kids to do the right thing, to act a certain way, and live a Christian life. But I guess you wouldn't get that, would you?" she scolded.

"Carla, it's okay to be mad, but don't insult me. I love that girl like my own. I'm not blessed with children, so I guess I should be careful what I say. I'm sorry. I'll make it right. You're always so happy around everybody else, but with me. . .you're always so quick to bite," Uncle Wit said.

"You had all those jobs before I was out of school. You boasted about all your experiences and all the things you learned, and you rubbed it in my face when I gave the slightest hint of being unsure. You said, 'Just try it, and you'll see if you like it.' You've never stayed a year at a job; where are you now?" she asked.

"Maybe I like trying new things," Wit said as he brushed Carla's shoulder in an attempt at a retreat.

Carla was happy, usually, but she would not have his disparaging remarks tear her daughter apart like he had done her for so many years while growing up, and she let him know on many occasions. He was much older than her, and she could not know what happened to him as a teen since their parents were very strict and private. But whatever it was, she didn't care.

Carrie's mother followed Wit a few steps behind. "You can do us all a favor and keep your ideas to yourself. Carrie doesn't need your worldly advice about life. I know you may mean well, but your past and ways of doing things have shown their compensation. You will do more harm than good with all the picking. I questioned myself for years about the things you said to me. Please, just let her be," Carla pleaded.

Uncle Wit finally removed himself from the grips of Carla's angry words and found Carrie on the back porch eating a bowl of ice cream with her friend, Zeb.

"Zeb, do you think I could have a word with Carrie? I have to leave in a minute," Uncle Wit asked.

"Sure, I'll be back in a bit, Carrie. There's a piece of cake in the house with your name on it, but I'm gonna eat it." He laughed.

Uncle Wit heard a large exhale from Carrie. "Aw, Carrie, I'm leavin', but I have something to say first. I'm not going to ask you about your future any more. I know you don't like it. I'm proud you're my niece."

With that, the screen door shut, and she watched him pass along the stone path and around the corner. The screen surrounding the back porch was covered in mildew and looked foggy. *My future looks the same as that screen. . .unclear,* she thought.

A soft and pleasant voice filled her right ear as her grandmother said her name. "Carrie, might I have a word, Sweetie?" she asked.

"Hi, Grandma, sit down," Carrie answered. "Tell me anything you like."

"Thank you, Dear, let me ask you this. Do you know that I had the same difficulty when I was your age? And I didn't have the choices you do, today."

"I'm sure it was different," Carrie said.

"It was; all I could do was trust the skills my family laid out before me, many years before me. I would have failed without the knowledge of my family. I want you to think about where you came from; you have roots. When you know your roots, you'll really know who you are. You'll be able to see how your ancestors overcame the setbacks and obstacles. You'll just have to take the time to do it," her grandmother explained.

"Thank you, Grandma. I'll try to make the time, I love you," Carrie said as she reached for a hug. They shared a few more minutes of conversation and eventually embraced warmly again. Carrie sat by herself again wondering about her future. She did not want to think about the past, and thinking about the things before her wasn't as enjoyable as she had hoped.

Saturday morning came so quickly. The birthday party ran late, and many of the guests stayed later than her parents wished. But they were not rude people, and they continued to entertain as long as people remained at their home. The day would most certainly be spent cleaning the backyard. She kicked off her covers and tiptoed to the bathroom across the hall as the wooden floor was cold on her feet.

"Is that you, Carrie?" her mother called up from the kitchen.

"I'm in the bathroom, Mom; I'll be down after a bit," she called back.

"I've got breakfast for you, old lady," her mother said, laughing.

"Very funny; you're the only old lady around here," she answered back.

Carrie's mother was always cracking jokes and tried keeping life light. She talked to her children the same way she talked to the dogs and cats, and other animals at the shelter. . .a bubbly spirited speech that always sounded as if there was a smile on her mouth. She smiled most of the time. She was a good Christian woman who knew how to show love and compassion. Carrie's mother reminded her daily to look for those who hurt so Christ could show through. When it came to Uncle Wit, her mother was altogether different. She had a distain for him that most of the family could not figure out. At times, Carrie was not sure her mother knew the roots of it all. Her mother seemed to have a sense of permission to attack him at the slightest incongruity concerning family customs. She would debate his every word and declare him incompetent in life's challenges. Her actions would play havoc on Carrie's relationship with him.

"Let me in there, Carrie, I have to go!" her little brother ordered. He rammed his shoulder into the door and rattled it. Carrie waited for the right moment as he hit the door hard and loud. She knew another one was coming. She threw the door open with perfect timing to witness a small boy of eight crash to the floor in a heap. The rug slid under him, and he was propelled into the far wall headfirst.

"Ha ha ha!" Carrie laughed. "I had no choice; you were going to break the door, Pete. Anyway, you get what you deserve."

Pete picked himself up off the floor and ran at her. She closed the door just in time to hear another loud thud. This time on the inside of the door. She held the knob tightly as he tried to turn it. Eventually, Carrie heard the telltale sign of his busy work and let go.

"If you two don't stop banging the bathroom door, I'll throw you in the kennel!" their father yelled from their parent's bedroom.

Her father was a kind person; he would not do such a thing, but he would discipline his children when needed, and they both knew it. It was a warning they heeded.

Carrie melted into the kitchen chair and shrugged as if another day would exhaust her.

"You know, Carrie, I heard about a job opening at the children's daycare on the corner of Eighteenth Avenue and Fourth Street. Have you ever considered taking care of little kids? It would be like taking care of the animals at the shelter. You just don't have to pet them as much there," her mother said with a smirk.

Her mother was still cooking a nice breakfast of sausage and eggs with biscuits as Carrie replied, "Very funny, Mom. I would not want to change diapers on little babies. I don't even like cleaning the dog. . .well, you know."

"It would be different, sweetheart, you know that."

"How would it be different, mom? They're both messes that smell."

"Well, for one," her mother said, "you don't have to use a shovel."

"Mom, you're too funny. I think I'll fill out an application at the mall for that cleaning position Teresa's mom told me about last night. Then I can talk to my friends when they show up there. I can also see when the new stuff comes out."

"Zeb called this morning. I told him he could go along with you today," her mother said.

"Mom, I can get a job on my own."

"I know, sweetheart, but wouldn't it be fun with a friend? He knows a lot of people, ya know. I told him you'd call."

"Okay, Mom, I'll call him," Carrie said a bit bleakly.

Carrie had a lot of friends. She thought of herself as an average-looking girl with light-colored hair and a nice smile, and knew that she could get a job on her merit. Her teeth were mostly straight and white, and her natural color was a light golden tan. She was known at her school for kindness, and she received the superlative award and was pictured in the high school yearbook. She was five feet, six inches tall, so she didn't stand out as the tallest student, but she was certainly not short for her age. Carrie was extremely popular in school with the girls, but not for the reasons one would expect. She had a steadfastness that preempted any engagement with the boys. The boys called her "No-No," and it got her respect among the girls in her immediate social group. It was a nickname she wore with pride. . .most of the time. But, it was also a badge of honor she earned by refusing the boys' advances, even when they were teasing her. In the boys' chatter to each other, they were told not to bother asking her out, she would just say, "no."

CHAPTER 2

Job Hunt

Carrie ate her breakfast quietly, helped with the dishes, and then readied herself in her bedroom for the day. As she arrived in the backyard, her father was nearly finished with the clean-up.

"Dad, I thought we were going to do this together. I can't believe you did it all," she complained.

"Well, no sense in ruining your birthday with a clean-up job; go have some fun with your mom in your new car. You've got your license now, so you'll need the practice with the car," her father said.

"Well, Dad, I was going to let Zeb go with me today after we cleaned up. He's coming over at eleven today. Mom told me she wanted to clean out her closet," Carrie cautiously said.

"Okay, baby," he said, "just be careful. At least I trust old Zeb. He's a good guy. You've not driven a lot, so be careful." Carrie nodded her head in agreement. "Oh, and Carrie," her father added, "present yourself with confidence. People like to see a well-spoken person, especially applying for a job."

Carrie thanked her dad with a big kiss, and she left using her cell phone. She contacted Zeb again in a text message, and he replied that he would be headed in that direction shortly. Carrie ran upstairs to check her hair and face. She stood in front of the mirror contemplating what she saw. She was thankful Zeb was coming over, but she questioned why she needed his help filling out job applications. Her feelings of inadequacy returned, and she recalled herself sitting on the porch swing yesterday before her party. She hated feeling like that, and now she would have to explain things to Zeb because he would see right through her emotions. He had the gift of discernment, and as should be, he kept everything confidential. She knew she was in good hands with Zeb, but she couldn't seem to reconcile her mother's call to him, and she did not want to ask Zeb the reason. She felt a little untrusted.

"Where do you want to go, Carrie?" Zeb questioned from the window of his old truck. "I think I'll take you to the mall first; there's lots of stores there."

"Yes, that's fine," Carrie replied. "I'm sure there's a store I'm not thinking about that might interest me. I'm just not sure. Oh, and we'll be taking my car, so park that old truck and get in my new ride."

Zeb did as she asked and overly tightened his seatbelt in a theatrical fashion as to make a point about her driving. Carrie rolled her eyes at him as she shifted into reverse.

As happy as they were, the drive became quiet, and Zeb could see Carrie's countenance change to worry. Usually, she talked his ear off in the car, and Zeb learned a lot about her when they were together. They had been friends forever.

Several miles later, Zeb asked her to pull into a parking lot. "I want to tell you something face to face."

"Here?" she asked.

"Yes, just up there in that parking lot." Zeb pointed.

Carrie agreed, but she knew she was going to get an earful from him. She readied herself with confidence as she made a small right turn, put the car in park, and turned to look at him with interest. Zeb rolled his window down for some fresh air and looked at her.

"Don't get mad. . ."

"I know," she interrupted, "I'm worrying again."

"No, no, no, let me finish," he said. "I want you to know that I talked to your mother at your birthday party. I overheard her talking to Wit," Zeb said.

"Are you kidding me? You talked with her this morning, too. I'm starting to think somebody doesn't trust me," Carrie said.

"No, you didn't let me finish. I thought she was a little hard on your uncle. I just asked her a couple of questions about the argument. . .but she didn't like that too much. She thinks I'm too young to understand I guess. I wanted her to know that you'll feel the same way about him if she kept leading you in that direction, but I couldn't find a way to say it. But, I do think he's good for you. I don't want you to be disrespectful to him. I get the sense he's had a rough time of it," Zeb said.

Carrie thought a good amount of time before she answered him. "So, you think my uncle, Wit, is good for me? He bugs me so much, Zeb, but I have a lot of fun with him, too. You have no idea," she said. "Sometimes the things he does are so funny and exciting, and other times I want to. . ."

"Carrie, there is something going on with your Uncle; I'm just not sure what it is. I wouldn't be surprised to learn he's a little depressed, disheartened. . .or something. But, he makes you think, and think deeply. I know he doesn't understand how things bother you, but he sure makes you think. He does care about you," Zeb said.

"My mother sure doesn't like him. He wants me to find a career out there right away, but I think Mom wants me to take my time on account of him. She'll tell me the exact opposite of what Uncle Wit says just for spite," Carrie said.

"Carrie, you're just seventeen years old, and you and I have been friends for a long time. I saw you sitting on the porch by yourself on your big day. I know what you were thinking; you didn't even see me walk by. We've talked about your future for only about a month, but I know your Uncle Wit bugs you about it all the time. There's no hurry to find your place in life. You think everything has to be finalized this very moment because he says so. Don't worry about what everybody is telling you," Zeb said. He eased back in the bucket seat. "You can always listen to advice, but you don't have to act on it. Have you tried praying about this?" Carrie shook her head. "You can work at a job for the fun and money right now, but you don't have to make it a career. Pick a place you think you can enjoy and earn a little money. If you pray about this, I know the right job will open up for you. Maybe we should pray now before we even start," he said.

"Well, how can you say my Uncle Wit is good for me and tell me not to listen to what others are telling me? That doesn't seem to make sense," she said.

"I think your Uncle Wit makes you think; I just want you to take it in the right direction. He means well with you. When he asks you these hard questions, it's not to pick. I truly believe he's sorry that he never settled down. He wants all things good for you," Zeb said. "Like I said, you can always listen to advice from people, that's respectful, but you don't have to follow it, including mine," he added. "However, I'd always take the advice to pray."

"Zeb, you're right. . .but pray. . .here in the parking lot? What if people come by and see us?" she asked as she surveyed the area.

"Carrie!" he said with surprise. "You know me, it doesn't matter what people think; maybe they'll be blessed, too. I pray with people at the dentist's office all the time, especially when they're hurting. And, there's really nobody here anyways."

Zeb took her hand and calmly bowed his head. Zeb looked up at her with one eye and said, "You, too."

Then he began, "Dear Lord, thank you for a great day. Thanks for a good friend in Carrie. Please go with us, today, as Carrie looks for a job. I pray, Lord, that Carrie can find happiness in this life as she works to begin a life that is centered on you. Lord, we trust you and place it all in your hands. . ."

Zeb continued his prayer and ended it on a beautiful note of forgiveness and promise.

Carrie lifted her head. "That made me feel funny inside, Zeb. That's a lot to ask God just for me."

"I told your mother I would help you the best way I knew how. You're one of my best friends. Do you remember when we went to the county fair in Lockton? I got lost. I was nine or ten, and you were eight. You found a police officer and immediately reported me missing. I remember the policewoman saying, 'You can't outrun the radio, son. Good thing your friend reported you; you were headed in the wrong direction.' I was desperately trying to find my way, and you made the difference that day," Zeb said. "I have never forgotten that."

Carrie knew he thought a lot about her. The bonds between the families were strong. Zeb and Carrie's parents were friends in college, and the couples continued their friendship, shared in each other's weddings, and joined the same church while Zeb's mother was pregnant with him. Carrie came along a couple of years later, and many playdates happened through the years. He was like an older brother to her.

"Well, I was worried about you, and that's all I knew to do. But promise me you'll leave my mother out of this stuff for now. You can look after me, but let's keep things between us," Carrie said.

"Okay, okay, I can do that, but don't forget, Carrie, I've always said your past will help you find yourself. You need to come over, and we'll check out your distant roots on my ancestry search pages online. You'll see what your ancestors did. Maybe that will help you find what you're good at. I've heard your dad say a few things," Zeb said.

"I think you've been talking to my grandmother; she said the same thing. But, I don't want to be a baker, a candlestick maker, or a common laborer," she said. "I've seen the old photographs."

"Oh, Carrie, you are so wrong. I said your past will help you find yourself, not how to be a candlestick maker. You have the wrong impression of an ancestry search. Your roots are so intertwined with time and place that you'll have to see it to believe it. I know you; you'll get bored, and when you do, you'll want to look. I'll be waiting," Zeb said.

"Okay, if I get bored we'll do it, but don't forget, you said you'd take me to the hot air balloon festival in a few weeks at Ditmar's Orchard, remember?" Carrie said.

"I know, but that is never a sure thing on account of the wind forecast, but we'll see. Just be thinking about what I said," Zeb motivated.

For several days, Zeb rode with Carrie to a number of places to drop applications. His work schedule at the dental office was lax, and he had called several of his coworkers to cover for him. But the situation could not last forever, and Zeb was forced to return to his schedule. Carrie could only drop off applications after school and on weekends. Young people and assistant managers were the only people she saw.

At a jewelry store, several snotty girls exaggerated their speech and actions. "Can we help you?" they said with disrespect and mocking in their voices.

"I would like to apply for a job here if that would be okay," Carrie said.

"Well, we don't really have any openings right now," one girl said.

Carrie immediately understood the condescending tone. The girls were dressed beautifully and adorned with jewelry obviously borrowed from the store's racks. She certainly was not their type and decided on the spot that she would not be happy working with such patronizing people. Carrie always had an incredible gift for dialogue and it came in handy. She pressed the issue with a little white lie to make them feel uncomfortable. It was payback; she was not in the mood for rudeness. "Your boss told me to bring my application back. Didn't she tell you? She said the girls in charge would know what to do. Aren't you the girls in charge? On second thought, I'll call her to see who she was talking about and clarify it with your boss tomorrow," Carrie said rather seriously.

"Oh, yes, now I remember. She told me you would be here. Here, I'll take that," one of the girls said.

"Oh, that's okay, I'll come back tomorrow afternoon and let her know you didn't know what to do," Carrie said as she walked towards the exit. She watched as the girls grinned heavily forced smiles of worry across their lipsticked faces.

She began to think that speaking with the owners or managers of the shops she had visited would somehow make all the difference. She hatched a plan to call in sick from school and visit these stores and shops personally. She launched her plan on a Tuesday. Zeb was not informed, neither were her parents. *I am a pleasant person, fair looking, I'm neat and clean, and I speak well,* she thought. *Surely I can get a job on my own merit. I just have to talk with the person that matters.* And she did just that in the morning and afternoon on a school day. Carrie visited nine shops at the mall, all the ones she had visited before, except for two, an ice cream shop and a shoe store. She didn't leave out the jewelry store, but only to share the girls' rudeness days before.

"Mom!" Carrie yelled from her downed window. "Hey, Mom, I got one. I got a job, Mom!"

Carla was cleaning the windows of the shelter and immediately climbed down off the ladder and ran to her daughter in the parking lot. "Carrie, it's two o'clock in the afternoon. Why aren't you in school? I mean, I heard you, but you're not in school! Did you skip school without permission?"

"Oh, Mom, it's okay. I got a job on my own. And I didn't go somewhere Zeb said to go," Carrie said excitedly.

"Where did you go?" her mother asked.

"I went everywhere I did before, but I talked with the people in charge this time, and it worked. I got a job at Arley's Ice Cream and Cone," she said.

"Well, great, but we'll talk at home about the truancy. I'm not writing you a note to save your hide. Figure that one for yourself, young lady! When you get home, lay your keys on the table," her Mother ordered.

"Mom, aren't you happ—"

Carrie was interrupted by her angry mother. "This is exactly what I was worried about. You just don't think things through. Do what I asked you to do, and do it now," she said angrily.

It was not the reaction she had hoped for. She was trying to make adult decisions, do things on her own, and make the people around her stop asking questions about her future. *They all want to know what I'm going to do with my life, but when I step out and do it, I'm punished,* she thought.

Somehow, Carrie would weather the next week or so; she knew her self-loathing days were over, for now, despite her punishment. The excitement of landing a job on her own took precedence over even this reality. She felt the disappointment in her mother's voice was unfortunate, but she could only think about her upcoming job when she would be serving ice cream to kids and families, and especially to her friends. The thoughts turned to boys, and she wished the nickname No-No would go away.

CHAPTER 3

Too Many Tasks

After a week of punishment, Carrie was still grounded from her car. The disappointment exaggerated by her mother was palpable. By Carrie's standards, her mother acted extremely heartbroken by the fact she would skip school using her newfound freedom. Carrie's mother had confessed that she feared a divergence in direction, and she would not let that become a foothold on her daughter. The punishment was harsh for a new teenage driver—two weeks without her car. Her mother held both sets of keys, and her only reprieves were a few times when her dad let her drive to the clinic. Her father loved being chauffeured around. A standing order to spend the evenings cleaning the clinic and preparing for the pickup of the euthanized animals hung on the fridge as a reminder of her afterschool duty—a job she hated. Carrie knew why she placed her there, even though her mother was blowing it all out of proportion. She wondered if her mother was displacing anger originating from her own childhood. Carrie presumed it had to do with Uncle Wit and the fact that she had made a bad decision that was characteristic of him.

In the middle of the second week, Carrie was still working evenings at the clinic. She began to think her father was getting a little weak in the knees over the length and severity of her punishment. With a fabricated tone in her voice she sweetly asked her father, "Dad, have you talked to Mom about me? Does she know I'm really sorry?" Carrie was cleaning out the medicine cabinet in the clinic's back room.

"Baby, it'll be over with soon; just do what you're told and it'll all pass. Punishment is not about forgiveness. Those concepts are far apart. Your mother and I forgive you, but you will pay the penalty for the wrong behavior," her Dad said.

"I know that, but have you asked her. . .I mean. . .really asked about me?" Carrie queried.

"Your mom and I have talked a little about it. I'll tell you, but it's between us. I'm not trying to go against your mother, now, but you understand, don't you? Well, anyway, we both think that your new car just got to your head, and the freedom it represented distorted your perspective," her dad explained.

It was not the response she was wanting, but she found an opening and decided to give it a try. She knew her father could draw up a truce between her and her mother and end the remaining time she was grounded from her car. She didn't want to be taken to her new job by her parents on Monday and Tuesday.

"I just wanted to make you proud. That was my only reason for doing it. I knew I could find a job by myself, but I knew what I had to do," she defended herself with the sweetest tone possible. "I'm not a little girl, and this punishment thing seems a little extreme if you ask me. I get that Mom's upset, but grounded for two weeks without the car you bought for me? I have to be allowed to make mistakes and pay for them myself, but two weeks? I just wish that Mom would understand," Carrie finished.

"Hold on there, Honey, you have to consider more than yourself in these matters. You didn't once consider how others would perceive the thing you did," her father said. "You skipped school. Anything could have happened to you, and we would never have known where you were. And, this is not just a mom thing; I support her decision with your punishment. . .because it was my idea," he said, pointing his finger at her.

"Oh. . .you're right, Dad, I'm sorry. It just seemed like an adult thing to do. I guess I didn't think about you guys because I was thinking about me too much. I have a problem that way, I guess," Carrie said sadly, trying to gain sympathy.

"Aw, now, like I said, it'll be over. It's already over in my mind, Carrie. I can't say that for your ma, but she'll understand that your lapse in judgement was just temporary. . .if it doesn't happen again, that is," her Dad said with a cocked head.

He smiled at her and left the area. Carrie noticed herself in a large mirror hanging by the back door. It showed her in full, from her head to her feet. She was mesmerized by what she saw. In the mirror's reflection hung a poster just over her head on the opposite wall. Captured in the picture was an elderly man with an aging dog. But the words at the top were backwards in the reflection. Rather than turn around, she carefully deduced the backward script into a meaningful sentence, "THE MOST DIFFICULT DECISION YOU WILL EVER HAVE TO MAKE."

Wow, she thought, *that's true. All my decisions are difficult; I wonder if the other girls feel like I do?* She knew the poster was for animal euthanasia, but the words stuck in mind and adhered to her soul. The girls at school, at least the ones she knew, seemed to have it all together. They talked about their freedoms and escapades outside of school. Many had just gotten great jobs at the popular clothing stores, or shoe stores, and they paraded around the school in their boasting attire. Some were set to follow in their parents' footsteps set up with future jobs in the family businesses. Carrie wanted nothing to do with the sadness and death of her family's business. She failed to see that several of these friends, the ones from her youth group and at school, were nearly a year ahead of her in age, but she looked to them for an example, nonetheless.

Carrie had not spoken to Zeb since the last time he accompanied her to the mall. She elected to sit in the back of the clinic van on a small jump seat as her father drove home. She finally called Zeb and told him the news. He sounded extremely disappointed in her by the words he used. "Carrie, I don't know why you would do something like that. In fact, I can't believe you skipped school. I would've grounded you, too," he said. "Nobody knew where you were."

"You sound like my Dad," she said sadly. "I think they just want me to work in that clinic for the rest of my life. That's why they're keeping this punishment thing going."

"I know you don't want anything to do with the clinic. I also told you to find a fun job just for the money, which you did, but in the meantime, try the ancestry search I told you about the other day. Find your roots, Carrie. You may find some interesting facts about yourself. Your roots are valuable. They tell you where your family's been and why you're who you are. You're a result of those who have gone before," Zeb said.

"I'm just going to have fun serving ice cream for now," Carrie said.

"Sure, but eventually you'll start questioning yourself. I know you. You will not be happy for long. You'll humble yourself into action. Your roots will make you do it. So, find out what your ancestors did. You may have skills like they did," Zeb said.

"One day I'll look 'em up, Zeb, but right now I have to get my car back," Carrie said.

The evening supper was quiet for a Friday. It was later than usual since she had been working with her father after school. She didn't care for the meal being served, but she guessed her mother already knew that. The bubbly personality seemed forced by her mother, but eventually, Carrie spoke to her.

"Mom, I have to start my new job on Monday after school, and I need my car if I'm going to work it out. Would you be willing to let me drive there? It would only be two days early. I told you I was sorry for everything. I wasn't going to run away. I'm not that type of person, Mom," Carrie said.

"Yes, you can drive again Monday, and I know who you are. You're just like your Uncle Wit," she said quietly.

"What?! What did you say, Mom?" Carrie asked.

"Well, now, don't get upset," her mother said. "My brother did that stuff to our parents for years. Always keepin' 'em guessing. I don't think you're too far removed from your roots, little girl," her mother said. "Your roots are tangled with his for sure."

"Little girl? Is that what you think of me? A little girl? I knew it," Carrie said in a slightly disrespectful tone.

"It's just an expression of affection, Carrie. Calm down," her mother said.

"Mom, I'm starting a new job Monday. That should mean something to you. I'm really a. . .well. . .big girl if you ask me," Carrie said.

Her mother was now trying to hide a smile. Carrie then assumed her mother was just trying to get under her skin, but she knew there was a truth in every statement.

"Mom, turn around. I want to see your face," she said as she threw her cloth napkin at her.

"You liked that part about Uncle Wit, didn't you?" her mother said. "Oh, and Carrie, Zeb thinks he's good for you, too."

Carrie grabbed her phone and rolled her eyes at her mother. Her father sat in the silence of strength, watching the whole thing. He continued eating his pigs-in-the-blanket, but Carrie saw him wink and nod at her mother. Her brother Pete had his earpods in with YouTube playing on his iPad. She gave her dad a small loving punch to the arm as she left, and he overreacted as if he would fall from his chair and laughed with his mouth full. "You're as mean as that old pitbull we got today."

Carrie whisked up the stairs as fast as happy could take her. She shed her dirty clothes and grabbed her favorite pajama bottoms and an older top from the drawer. She ran to the bathroom to ready herself for bed as usual. Her eyeliner had run below her left eye, and it reminded her of a sad clown. She pictured herself as a runaway in a circus eking out a living any way she could. And in her head, a sentence was running through, "You're just like your Uncle Wit. You're just like your Uncle Wit." Joining the circus was something her uncle would probably do. Now she questioned if her mother was just goofing around or was actually stating a truth. *People often say things in jest when they mean it another way,* she thought. She was poring over the last interactions she had with Uncle Wit. She thought about her first job and what that would be like. *Could she scoop ice cream properly? Would she be liked?* Her thoughts were everywhere as she washed her face and combed her hair. Finally finished with the nightly routine, faster than it had ever been completed before, she settled down with her English book from school and began a writing assignment. *It's due Monday,* she thought.

Spurred on from the conversation earlier, she could not believe what her hand was writing across the top of the paper. "This is a great title," she said outloud. Finding words she had never used before, the paper took on a deeper meaning—much deeper than could have been imagined. The ideas were bringing clarity to her self-awareness, but ambiguity to why it was on the paper in the first place. *Maybe I'm just tired,* she thought, but she continued to embellish the composition with amazing ease and understanding. As she read it back to herself, it sounded reasonable. Slowly her eyelids became heavy, and she felt her head bob a few times. It wasn't long before she slumped forward and fell on her side fast asleep, her English book and paper displayed on top of the blanket.

Making the nightly rounds, her mother came in to say good night since light was spilling out from under Carrie's bedroom door. Noticing her child asleep, she moved to cover her. She placed her English book on the desk next to the bed, but the paper slid out and fluttered to the floor. She reached and picked it up. She read it all. Slowly, tears welled up in her eyes as the words illuminated Carrie's thoughts. Her hands began to shake, and she stood motionless looking at her dreamy little girl of seventeen. She stared. She stood. Her hands continued to shake. She recalled the countless "Good nights," and the *Don't Let the Bed Bugs Bite* poem she had shared with her daughter. She remembered the *Now I Lay Me Down to Sleep* prayer and how she tucked her in tightly each night. She managed a smile and laid the paper on the book then backed out of the bedroom as if threatened by an unseen force. She snapped off the light, and ran down the hall to her husband. Collapsing in his arms as he stood by the dresser removing his tie, she sobbed and mumbled words that were hard to make out.

"Honey, is everything okay, baby, what's wrong, what's wrong?" he asked as he stood her up. Through the tears, she explained about a paper she had just read in Carrie's bedroom. Allen seemed to immediately understand the contention as he placed his arm lovingly around her.

Allen held her until she fell silent. Finally settled, Carla expressed regret for acting in such a way. "I'll speak to her tomorrow," she said.

"Honey, do you want to talk about what the paper said?" he asked.

"It's nothing, Allen, I'm just tired and emotional; I'll be alright. But we need to pray for her," she said.

"Carla, we pray for our children a lot, but I think I want to pray for you tonight," Allen said.

Carrie was not informed about her mother reading the essay. The weekend was progressing along just fine, and Carrie was in Sunday school listening to Zeb share a story from Job 14. The verses, seven through nine, caught her attention as it seemed they were directed toward her. Carrie had been considering the ancestral search that Zeb had suggested, and the scriptures reminded her of it.

For there is hope for a tree, when it is cut down,
That it will sprout again, and its shoots will not
fail. Though its roots grow old in the ground and
its stump dries in the soil, at the scent of water
it will flourish and put forth sprigs like a plant.

Zeb had studied the Bible for years and considered a degree in pastoral ministries. His ease at learning gave him an advantage, yet he decided to focus on a career in dentistry. He was already working at a dental office which helped promote his knowledge, but because of his Biblical knowledge and faith, he was offered a teaching position for Carrie's Sunday school class.

Having listened to Zeb for most of the lesson, she knew the scriptures in Chapter Fourteen were about Job's questions about the death of man, and man's final destination, but the two verses were captured in her mind, and she just knew Zeb was thinking about her as he read them. He continued discussing Job's miserable friends. Carrie was fortunate to have a friend like Zeb, and she let him know after class.

"Zeb, I want you to know how much I appreciate you. You make me think. I like that. I don't always think things through, ya know," Carrie said.

"Wow, what brought that on?" Zeb asked.

"I just want you to know that I'm thinking about getting with you on the ancestral search. I'm just not ready for that yet. I start my new job tomorrow after school, so I'm going to focus on that for a while," she said. "I know my roots will still be there when I do."

"Very funny, Carrie," he said rolling his eyes. "Your roots should have been looked at before you went job hunting. I'm telling you, finding out about your roots will give you ideas and courage."

Despite her refusal for the ancestral research, Zeb seemed proud as they walked together with friends to the sanctuary for Sunday service. Later they all gathered at a local diner, and Carrie finally shared the good news about her ice cream scooping job.

Carrie awoke Monday morning with a new eagerness; she had a reason to exist in her mind. She would serve ice cream to the children of Council Bluffs. Unfortunately, it would be after school and only three times a week. Carrie envisioned buying her own ice cream store one day, but for now, she would have to get out of bed, dress for the part, and make her way to school where she would make sure to spread the word about her whereabouts later in the evening.

It was a long Monday at school. Math class made her head hurt, and English simply wore her out. Her English assignment was a hard task in her mind, and she wasn't even sure why she chose the topic heading for her paper. She seemed confused about how to end it and barely wrote a word the whole hour.

"Carrie, I gave you that assignment Friday, remember?" said her teacher, Mrs. Brozer.

"I just need one more day to finish, Mrs. B.," Carrie pleaded.

"I will expect it tomorrow with today's assignment then," her teacher said.

"Thank you so much. I'll have it," Carrie said.

Her Economics class gave her some ideas about the real possibilities of owning her own ice cream shop. *It would be called Ice Cream World. What a great name,* she thought. She would place a store in every town across America with large yellow and red letters overhead. She would be the Willy Wonka of ice cream. . .until she heard a strangely familiar call.

"Carrie. . . Carrie! It's your turn to read, Carrie. Pay attention to what we're doing please!" her teacher said with a harsh tone.

"I. . .I. . .I don't know where we are, sir. I'm sorry."

"Top of page ninety-four, please. See me after class as well," he said.

Carrie was totally embarrassed, and several snickers were heard at her expense. After class, Carrie listened to her teacher amble through topics of attentiveness, extra grade opportunities, and study habits in his class. It was all stuff she had heard before. She apologized once more and tried to leave.

"Oh, Carrie," he said, "I hear you're going to be serving ice cream at Arley's now. Is that true?"

"Yes, sir, it is," she said.

"Good, I'll be by eventually. That's my favorite place," he said.

Oh, brother, she thought as she left his class. *I hope he doesn't come on my first day.*

Carrie headed to her honors History class. She was celebrated in the class as the walking historic dictionary. Her school was one of only five in the area to have honors History. The focus was usually political history, but the students discussed all relevant areas including debate. She was not on the debate team but helped the others train. Carrie could take either side of an argument and usually win. But history was her favorite subject, and the books in her bedroom were testament to that.

Her last class was P.E. She didn't like it due to the large number of males in the class. Many of the boys were not Christian in their language. Much of the time the boys stood around and talked about inappropriate things; many times it seemed as if she was back in middle school, but the comments were more sophisticated and largely innuendo. Carrie was mostly left alone because she simply shared with the teacher when it happened. She could do it without sounding like an informant, and most knew not to confront her about such things, but it didn't mean she couldn't hear it happening around her.

On one occasion, Carrie took up for a new student from another state. The boys had berated the girl for her different dress and accent through the use of innuendo and social rejection. Having come from a very conservative area, Beth, the new girl, was beside herself and nearly crying when Carrie intervened.

"Hey!" Carrie said. "How old are you? You're acting like middle school students; can't you see you're tormenting her? Is that what a man would do? You have no right. Grow up!"

The comments were so compelling, one teen boy found his way to Beth and apologized to her. The others turned and left due to Carrie's reputation for reporting and debate, but it was a reputation she was proud of, especially in moments just like that. As a result, Beth became a close friend and a member of her youth group at church. With some urging from Carrie, Beth received Christ and was baptized later that month.

The drive to the ice cream shop took forever. Traffic was crazy, and Carrie beat on her steering wheel at each red light. "Please, God, let me get there on time and in one piece," she said. She had run laps around the football field during P.E. and now was feeling a little stuffy, maybe even sick. She put it out of her mind as she sniffled slightly, and her ears popped. She was determined not to be sick on her first day on the job.

She waited patiently in the blue and green tiled store. The other employees prepared for departure, and she knew her time was coming.

"Hello, Carrie," Mr. Gibson finally greeted. "Are you ready for your training day?"

"Well, yes, I am," she said with her hands on her hips. Carrie could feel any last dollops of depression lingering in the back of her mind leave. It dawned on her that the last few weeks had been relatively sadness free all on account of this very moment, notwithstanding her punishment.

"Great. Then let's start with a tour of the back room," he said.

Carrie was shown everything. She loved the large walk-in cooler and the racks where he stored all the ice cream. There were many flavors, and each one had its own spot. He showed her how to scoop the ice cream and how to wash the dishes. She was shown how to keep hot water in the spoon-cup to help the scooper glide through the frozen cream. She knew she could run that shop, even if Mr. Gibson had to leave for a while. She especially loved the cash register and how adult it made her feel. She had a sense of responsibility, and it felt good.

Her first customer was a small boy of five and a man with a large mustache. She laughed to herself as the man painted his mustache with mint chocolate chip ice cream. The little boy received only one scoop, but his Dad had three. She finally handed him a napkin with a smile, and Mr. Gibson nodded his approval.

At 9:00 p.m. Carrie was still in her room crying. Her mother could not take it anymore. She had frightened her little brother, Pete, with her actions. And despite storming into the house and running to her room with the words, "Don't ask!" being the only thing she said, her mother slowly opened the door and asked the obvious question.

"Mom, I can't talk right now; you should leave."

Her mother stepped into the room and quietly closed the door and began, "Sweetheart, what is going on? Did you go to your new job? You forgot, didn't you? Are you upset because you forgot about going to work?" she asked.

"No, Mom, I went and don't ever want to go in there again!" Carrie murmured through her pillow. Carrie was lying face down on her bed, shoes on, and a blue apron still tied around her waist.

"Carrie, turn over and tell me what happened," her mother ordered.

"I had to run laps around the football field for Gym class today. It was cold outside, and now I'm sick."

"Well, did the owner make you go home?" her mother asked.

"No, Mom, he fired me!" Carrie cried and turned her face into the green floral pillow again.

"He fired you for being sick? That's crazy," her mother said.

"Mom, he didn't fire me for being sick; he fired me for sneezing in the ice cream buckets in front of customers."

"Oh, Carrie, you didn't!"

"It's all Mr. Pelt's fault for making us run laps in the cold air. Now I have a cold," Carrie complained in a nasally tone.

"Couldn't you have turned your head or caught a Kleenex or something?" her mother asked.

"It came so fast. I had no time. Mr. Gibson yelled at me and had to close the shop. He made me take out two buckets and throw them away. I felt so bad, Mom. I was crying, and he was still yelling, 'You cost me hundreds!' My teacher was there with his little girl, Mom. I was so embarrassed! Please just let me be now, okay, Mom?" she asked.

"I'll leave you, but I'm going to have my say. First, let me just say that what you did was very immature, and you know that we've had this talk before. You usually do well around others outside of this home, but you act like a little girl around here much of the time. Maybe it's me, maybe I haven't taught you independence like I should have. Whatever it is, it's your turn to act your age. Even now, Carrie, this is something I told you when you were twelve, and I'm getting tired of it. Secondly—" Her mother stopped as she was interrupted.

"Mom, I get what—" Carrie was cut off by her mother.

"You will let me finish. . .secondly," she said boldly, "I want you to consider how your actions will affect others. Think things through, Carrie. When I bought that car, I just knew you would do something thoughtless with it, and I was right. Then, I let you out of your punishment early, and for what? Well, you finally got what you were asking for. I suggest you go to bed and think hard about changing some things; you're seventeen, and it's time!" her mother demanded.

"Carla, you in there?" Her father was lightly knocking on the door. "Carrie, everything okay?" he asked, still knocking.

"You can stay home from school tomorrow, Carrie," her mother said, walking to the door. "I think you're going to be sicker in the morning from all that crying. I understand you're upset, but don't forget to say a prayer tonight, and really ask God for direction, Carrie." She opened the door for her husband and took his hand. Carla attempted to lead him away, but he stopped and walked into Carrie's room.

"Can I pray with you, sweetheart?" her father asked. "Life can be rough just starting out, but we can always ask for direction. It's never too late."

"I'll be fine, Dad. I was just so embarrassed. That's the only reason I'm upset; just embarrassed," Carrie said.

Carla came back into the room and stood behind Allen with her eyes toward the floor. There was a long pause before anyone spoke again. "Your mother suggested you stay home from school tomorrow. That's fine by me, but I want you down at the clinic by ten tomorrow morning. We can talk then. Now, try to get some sleep. We all make mistakes, but at least we learn what not to do," her father said. Carrie's parents made their way through the door and shut it quietly.

"You should have prayed with her, Carla. She needed you," her father said.

"I will see her in the morning, Allen. Come, I'll tell you what happened; you won't believe it," her mother said.

As the hall cleared, Pete snuck in and lay down beside her. He was unsure what had happened but placed his little arm over his sniffling older sister. His voice was soft and sweet, unlike a bratty little brother. "I still love you, Carrie. Don't cry," he said. She rolled over and met his eyes. "I love you, too," she cried. Pete lay motionless beside her for some time, and Carrie drank up the attention from him. He finally closed his eyes and fell asleep. It was exactly what she needed, a snuggle of love and understanding, and it was Pete in his innocence who provided it. Even still, Carrie lay adding to her self-derogating framework and questioned her failed attempts at adultness.

CHAPTER 4

Hot Air

The rest of the week was hard on Carrie and her mother's relationship. They barely spoke. Carrie could feel the want in her mother for a small conversation, but it never happened. Carrie filled her mind with quick retorts to any semblance of questioning coming from her mother about the ice cream fiasco. Everything from "Hold on a second Mom, I'll be right back," to "Can I ask you a question?" Anything worked as long as it changed the subject. She was just not ready to discuss the most embarrassing moment of her life.

Saturday mornings at the Barclay's usually started early. Carrie's mother would have a good breakfast cooking, and her father was already in the yard or garage working on a project of some magnitude. Her brother could be found watching cartoons on T.V., with his high-pitched laughter serving as an alarm clock for Carrie, but it was not that way this Saturday. Her father was nowhere to be found, and she had noticed her mother from her bedroom window talking to a neighbor by the front mailbox. She could imagine her mother spilling the beans about her time

Monday night. Before she had gotten up, she lay in her bed for a while, thinking about her little brother who had slept so innocently next to her Monday night. She remembered his impassioned effort to soothe her discomfort. *What a great little kid,* she thought.

It was the mirror in the bathroom that made her remember the poster at the clinic. She stared into her own eyes not really recognizing who was looking back. That human figure turned to a stranger for a moment. She realized that she was looking at a reverse image. "This is not really me," she said aloud, "I'm the opposite of this." The poster from the clinic came to the forefront of her thought. "THE MOST DIFFICULT DECISION YOU WILL EVER HAVE TO MAKE." She could not shake the thought. Then, as if clouds rolled back like a scroll, she saw it—a mental image outlined in gold sparkling sequins. It flashed like a neon sign in her mind—*THE MOST NECESSARY DECISION YOU WILL EVER HAVE TO MAKE.* "That's it!" she said. "I know what I have to do." She knew she was still too young. . .young in actions and deeds, that is. She had cried herself to sleep, daydreamed in school, skipped school altogether, and acted irresponsibly. She felt small, and embarrassed; she felt like a little kid for acting like she had with her mother. She reminisced about her mirror antics when just a child, and how she would hold her hair up behind her head and turn this way and that. She recalled how she imagined an older Carrie, a more responsible Carrie, a daughter her parents would be proud of someday, but that time was now here, and she was disappointing them and herself. She raised up on her tippy toes once more, remembering how she pranced back and forth before the mirror trying to look older and more sophisticated. As she stood facing her opposite, another reminder of immaturity was realized; the backward letters on her pajamas, as revealed by the mirror, read, "Mommy's little girl." "Wow, I have some growing up to do," she said quietly as she came down onto her heels.

"Carrie, are you in there? I have to go!" Her little brother was up and to his usual self. But Carrie opened the door on his first knock and let him in. He stared at her as she walked out. "What?" he said in disbelief at the ease of what just happened.

"Oh, nothing," she said. "I'll use it when you're through."

It was Carrie's first act with her new determination—that necessary decision.

While getting dressed, a few questions raced through her head. "How will Mom trust me again?" "Why did I act so dumb?" "What does it really look like to be mature?" and "Will anyone notice?"

Carrie laughed, because she knew she had the answer to her last question by the look on her brother's face. It gave her the confidence to talk to her mother as she met her in the stairwell as she descended. Her mother looked a bit disheveled and different. Carrie could not discern the meaning of the change she saw; she had other pressing thoughts taking precedence of her time.

"Mom, I saw you outside this morning; is it cold?" she asked, avoiding any mention of their encounter Monday night. Still, she didn't want to talk about that with her newfound determination to move forward—not even five days later.

"It's a beautiful morning. I'd say sixty-five degrees already. Not a cloud in the sky. Oh, and by the way, the hot air balloon event has been approved this morning out at

Ditmar's Orchard," her mother said. "The neighbor just mentioned it to me."

"Oh, wow. Zeb was wanting to go to that," Carrie said.

"Well, you call him right now; you deserve a little break," her mother said.

Carrie knew that comment was a small insinuation. She was sure her mother wanted to talk about her job loss, but she would not comply with the request. Carrie imagined every comment as a request to discuss her ice cream debacle.

"I will, right after I eat a bite," Carrie said.

Carrie barely stopped while descending the stairwell, and her mother's head turned to follow her as she passed. Carrie didn't make eye contact. It was difficult and awkward for both of them, and Carrie heard a depressing sigh come from deep inside her mother's chest.

When she arrived in the kitchen, there was no sign of cooking. One cup sat empty on the counter with a tell-tale hint of white in the bottom. She realized that her mother had slept late; it was very much out of the ordinary. She then wondered where her father was, but not for long. There were indications he was at the clinic—no breakfast, the green truck gone, and his rubber boots were missing. He was spraying down the concrete kennels in the back of the clinic, she determined.

She grabbed a Pop-Tart from the cabinet and went out back to the screened porch. She phoned Zeb quickly, and still pondering those odd things, lifted the Pop-Tart to her ear. She laughed to herself. "I must be going crazy."

"Going crazy, what? I can barely hear you," a voice came from afar.

"Oh, Zeb, sorry, I was just talking to myself. You busy?" she asked.

"I'm still laying in the bed," he said.

"Well, you wanted to go to the balloon festival, didn't you? I'll drive," she said.

"I thought they were going to cancel due to the wind forecast," he said.

"Nope, they got it wrong again. It's on," Carrie proclaimed.

Zeb loved hot air balloons. His grandfather had one, and he remembered many fun times riding high in the red, yellow, and white striped one. Zeb had mentioned it to her on many occasions.

"Well, okay, I guess. I haven't done that since my grandfather died. Sounds fun. It'll bring back good memories. I'll be ready by the time you get here," he said.

Riding in the car always got Carrie talking. Zeb had often stated that to her. "You'll talk about anything, as long as you're riding down the road," he would say. And, he was right. The passing scenes relaxed her as if parts of her brain had turned off, and the other tranquil parts turned on. It was very hypnotic to Carrie, and she acted as if she was in therapy talking to Zeb. This ride was no different, and eventually she was able to share with Zeb the ice cream fiasco of that Monday night. She didn't get the usual understanding from him with stories such as this. Like a coin in a gumball machine, Carrie could consistently elicit loving and compassionate direction from him, then chew on it for the day. Usually it tasted good, and his advice was great. However, Carrie found Zeb laughing so hard that she felt like stopping the car and kicking him out.

"I'm sorry, Carrie, really, I am," Zeb said, still laughing. "I'm not laughing at you, just the scene. Mr. Gibson must have been so mad." He continued laughing.

Carrie finally smiled. "Well, it's a story I probably won't live down. My teacher, Mr. Luchsinger, is probably gonna tell everybody," she said with a small smile. "I owe Mr. Gibson a couple hundred dollars. I should probably pay him for the mess up," she said as her smile disappeared.

"Wow, that's a real adult thing to say," Zeb said.

"It is?" asked Carrie. "Well, yes, it is," she corrected. "I'm a little more mature as a result of that whole catastrophe. I've decided to do some things differently, Zeb."

Carrie was very proud of herself in the moment. Already, she had two adult decisions in a matter of an hour in her mind, and Zeb had easily recognized one. She trusted his appraisal.

They arrived at the balloon event in time to see the rising of the first three. One was the shape of Tweety Bird, one red and yellow striped, and one with a quilt-like pattern.

"Those are so beautiful. I saw the whole Looney Tunes gang of characters a couple of years ago in Georgia when I went to see my grandpa," Zeb said. "Let's get going. There's a lot to see."

They parked the car and gathered their things. "Zeb, can you carry my phone? I don't have any back pockets in these pants," Carrie asked.

"We won't need your phone. I have one if we do. Just leave it in the glove box and lock the doors," Zeb said.

Carrie made sure the doors were locked then looked at Zeb. "Mom was right. I needed this break. Thanks for going with me. You're such a good friend," Carrie said.

"You're welcome, Carrie. Just do me one favor. Tell your Mom what you just said. It'll make her feel good to know she's helping you," Zeb said.

Carrie agreed reluctantly, not wanting to give an inch in the ongoing dispute with her mother, but trusted Zeb's judgement. Still, Carrie wondered about the effects of sharing that with her mother. She knew her mother was right, yet she did not feel like giving her a compliment just yet.

Zeb and Carrie wandered around for an hour or so, bumping into school friends along the way. It was a great time under all the tall balloons, but it felt a bit strange to Carrie. She felt like she was on a date for some reason. She had no feelings for him like that, but she knew Zeb had once felt strongly about her. She also knew that he was going to ask her out when she was in sixth grade. The district schools in her area moved students to new school locations every two years. Seventh and eight were at the junior high school, ninth and tenth were at a downtown campus, and eleventh and twelfth were at the main high school just out of town, so they were always in different schools two years apart. It was not a good dating situation. Zeb had moved on, keeping his friendship with Carrie tight, and was happily dating a girl from Tama; she was half Meskwaki and lived in the Meskwaki Settlement in Tama County, a Native American community. Mary was absolutely beautiful, and Carrie was a little jealous of her since outings with Zeb were interrupted from time to time. She knew Zeb could tell this by the way she changed the subject each time her name came up, but Zeb didn't press her. There was something about Zeb that could not be explained, and Carrie loved him for his true friendship. Mary had gone west for the fall to stay with an ailing grandmother, so Carrie didn't feel bad about the day's excursion, but she could tell Zeb missed Mary considerably.

Plans were being made to find something to eat and eventually return home, but before she could tell Zeb what she was hungry for, cold hands wrapped around her eyes from behind, and a strange "Guess who?" was whispered in her ear.

"Oh!" she said startled. "Um, it's Matt. . .No, it's Gary. . . I give up," she said.

She pulled down on the hands and turned around to see her Uncle Wit. "Oh, it's you," she said rather dejectedly.

"Thanks," he said as he stepped back, wounded by the statement.

"Oh, I'm sorry, Uncle Wit, I didn't mean it like that." She giggled. "I just thought it was going to be someone I hadn't seen in a while, that's all," she said.

"Beautiful day!" he said.

"Yes, it is," Zeb returned.

"Zeb and I are just about to leave," Carrie said.

"You and Zeb had a good time, then?" They both nodded to him. "I'm going up in that balloon over there, the bright yellow one with the black checkers still on the ground," Uncle Wit said. "Hey, you want a ride? We might have room; it's a big one."

Carrie looked at Zeb. "Sure," Zeb said with enthusiasm.

"Great! I'll go check with the pilot to see if he's filled the rider's list. He's a great friend of mine; wait here," Wit said.

"Zeb, do you think it's safe?" Carrie asked.

"Of course, it's the twenty-first century, Carrie," Zeb said as they sat on a park bench.

After a few minutes, Uncle Wit returned, walking a little slower than usual. "Sorry, guys, they only have room for two more riders. I saved the spots, but I can only take one of you."

Zeb stood up and took Carrie's hand and raised her. "Carrie, you should go. I've ridden many times with my grandparents. I'll chase if it's not too far," Zeb said.

"I'm scared," Carrie said.

"Aw, it'll be fun," Uncle Wit said. "Zeb, the air is tracking nearly straight east, so ride along state Highway 6. We'll set down somewhere past Oakland, probably closer to Lewis. It's wide open out there. But, I better get over to the balloon. I'm Cremation Charlie," Uncle Wit said.

"What is that? Carrie asked.

Uncle Wit took off in a trot. "That's the guy who holds up the ripstop so it won't be burned while the air is heating in the envelope," Zeb said.

"What's ripstop?" Carrie asked.

"That's the balloon fabric. . .the envelope. You just go over there and watch; you'll learn a lot. I'll get some lunch and meet you over there," Zeb said.

Carrie weaved her way around the standing balloons. They were so flamboyant. People were jumping in their baskets and tossing sandbags off. Some were untying ropes and floating away with loud rushes of burning gas. The walk to the yellow balloon calmed her fears. It looked so scary before, but watching so many people with smiles and excitement helped. She arrived just in time to see the envelope lift off the ground and hang over the basket, wrinkly and wavy, with only half of it filled.

"It won't be long now, Carrie," Uncle Wit called loudly over the roar of the gas flames. "Go to Mag, the lady in the red hat, and sign your name under mine," he said.

Carrie found the lady as he asked, but she read the paperwork first. Uncle Wit had listed himself as custodial parent over her so she could ride with permission. She wondered what her mother would say if she saw it. Uncle Wit gave her a thumbs up as she deliberated on signing, and it was accompanied by a wink and a nod as he walked over to her.

"Uncle Wit?" she asked. "Do you think I should ask my mother, you know, call her first?"

"Well, now, Carrie, that depends. Are you old enough to make your own decisions or not?" he chided.

That poster phrase, "THE MOST DIFFICULT DECISION YOU WILL EVER HAVE TO MAKE," jumped in her head like popcorn. It bounced around for a while until she heard her name.

"Carrie, what do you want to do?" he asked.

Carrie thought, then began, "I want to make the adult decision—"

"Well, good," Uncle Wit interrupted, "then come on, we're almost ready. Sign your name first, and come on."

She felt rushed. She was going to say she should call her mother first, but that didn't feel adult-like, either. *When do I stop asking my mom's permission for my life?* she thought. *Come what may, making decisions was hard.* Her uncle's insistence, however, gave her a reprieve from the matter. She would mention the trip to her mother, but later in the next week, she decided. Zeb made it back just in time to hand her half of a sub sandwich and a can of Coke as the gondola lifted off the ground. "Thanks, Zeb. See you at the landing site," she yelled down to him.

It was her third adult decision for the day, but a nagging feeling in the back of her mind threatened to repeal her satisfaction. The present situation, however, quickly ended her internal debate.

Up they went. It was a rather quick ascent. The pilot did turn out to be a close friend to Uncle Wit. He already knew her name. "So, Carrie, what do you think of that little world down there?" Troy asked.

"Oh, it's so wonderful. It's so beautiful. I have never been this high, ever. I've never flown in a plane or anything," Carrie said.

"Well, you're in an aerostat," Troy said. "This rope controls that lever there and lets gas out to the burners. The burners warm the air. I descend by letting the air cool or opening the flap at the top called the parachute vent."

"How fast are we flying?" Carrie asked.

"The higher we go the faster we'll go, usually, but it all depends on the weather. We'll stay down low so the spotters can see us. I'm sorry your boyfriend couldn't go," Troy said.

Uncle Wit laughed. Carrie looked at him goofy-like and motioned for him to be quiet. She turned to see Council Bluffs fade away into small meaningless spots in the distance. Turning again, she saw the meaningless spots ahead arrange themselves into farms or small towns, and trees and cows. She witnessed the large birds of prey soaring around the other balloons in the distance, and she saw the small balloon shadows float across the ground below. It gave her a sense of the speed they were traveling. The sights caused a tiny stir of introspection, and she remembered that famous poem by T.R. Gunderson. She grabbed Uncle Wit's arm and said, "Listen to this poem. 'High on ends like birds we tend, to fly the day from the knowledge they lend. From man, our flights must atone, to the bird their home is not alone.'"

"Pretty nice there, girl," her uncle said.

"Just thinking about flying up here. You know, it seems peaceful here. Who would know all the trouble people face down there? I guess God would be the answer to that question," Carrie said as her hair whirled around and around.

"Carrie, I never really thought about it like that. I've been up here a lot with Troy but never gave it a thought," he said.

Another rider overheard their conversation and wanted to discuss the matter. "May I add to your conversation?" he asked.

"Sure," said Carrie.

"I'm a pastor from Omaha, and I heard your poem. It was beautiful. I have never heard it before. I also heard your question. It's funny, because I preached about that last Sunday. My sermon was from Isaiah 55:9. 'For as the heavens are higher than the earth, so are My ways higher than your ways and My thoughts than your thoughts.' "

"I've heard that scripture a lot. And it's true. Zeb, one of our chasers down there, always reminds me of that," Carrie said.

"So, you're Christian then?" asked the pastor.

"Yes, we are. . .well, I mean. . .I am," said Carrie. "Uncle Wit, you'll have to answer that question for yourself."

"Oh, I'm sorry, I wasn't listening. What was that?" Wit said.

"I didn't mean to butt into your conversation. I just wanted you both to know that God is not just watching us from a distance, like that song says, but God is watching, interacting, and guiding us in life. God bless both of you. Let's enjoy the view," he said. "Oh, and by the way, you should look up the song by Hillsong United, 'From God Above.' It's a great tune about Christ coming from God."

"I know that song!" Carrie said excitedly. Uncle Wit had lost interest in the conversation.

"Share it with your uncle, Carrie. I think he just might like it." He shook her hand, turned around, and continued a conversation with the other women accompanying him.

Uncle Wit twirled his finger around the side of his head as if to indicate crazy. Carrie grabbed his hand and stretched her eyes wide. "Stop that, you crazy man," she said. Uncle Wit grabbed her hand, pulled her closer, and gave her a little hug.

"I remember when you were a little girl; you couldn't get enough of my hugs," he said.

"That's because you always had candy in your coat pockets," Carrie said with a slight chuckle. "Maybe I should check them again."

"Ya know, I've been thinking, Carrie. All my life I've been trying things here. . .and there, just blowin' in the wind like this here balloon, but, I know I come from people who had a lot of talent. . .good people who made a difference, people who cared what they were doin'. I just never really got settled. I jumped from love to love, loving this and loving that. It just seemed so tangled in my mind. But, I have roots, by golly. And those roots are tangled, too. I guess you could say I come from tangled roots," Uncle Wit explained. "Tangled roots sure hold fast. Yep, I come from tangled roots." Uncle Wit got quiet as he seemed to contemplate what he had just said, but Carrie broke the silence between them.

"What does that mean?" she asked.

"It means that all those skills, motivations, wants, and desires your ancestors had are all instilled in you. They hold you together, and they anchor you so you know you'll never fail at what you try; you just decide something ain't for you," Uncle Wit said. "You'll make mistakes and try things that ain't you, but that's okay. You'll know when you find the right things. I just want you to find a bunch of 'em before you decide which is for you."

Carrie stayed quiet for a time and finally responded. "Uncle Wit, I've always been taught to trust the Lord for things I needed. You put all this in a worldly way; that's why you feel like you're drifting around. Your parents are good people, and you know why. Grandpa and Grandma are Christians; you were raised to believe. I so wish you could trust the Lord with your life. What happened to you?" Carrie asked.

Uncle Wit's eyes widened for a moment. "I had a lot of livin' to do, just wanted to be free to do what I wanted. No harm in that. I like finding new things to do and moving on to other things," he retorted.

"Yes, but that moving on thing doesn't do you any favors. And you still say that your roots are tangled, but with whom? Our ancestors, from what I've been told, were strong and resilient," Carrie said. "Maybe a few words with the Lord could make a difference."

Carrie was moved by her own comments. She knew more words with the Lord were always the answer to uncertainty, so she quietly recited the Lord 's Prayer in her mind.

Uncle Wit didn't answer and quickly pointed his attention towards Troy.

The pastor was listening despite the wind that whistled around everyone's ears.

"Mr. Wit, can I ask you a question, sir?" the pastor asked as he placed himself between Carrie and Uncle Wit.

"What do you need, Mister?" Uncle Wit said. Carrie turned to view the sights and lessen the attention on Uncle Wit. She seemed to understand where the pastor was going and assumed what the questions were going to be.

"Have you ever given God credit?" the pastor asked.

"Credit for what? Credit for a wandering life, credit for a loveless life, credit for a bad time in sch—"

Uncle Wit stopped short of his last comment, but quickly added. "Yeah, I've given Him credit for all of it. Isn't it He who designed my life like this? Yeah, He gets all the credit. I even had Christian parents; that worked out so well. Ever tried livin' up to perfect parent expectations? Is that what you want to hear, Mister?" Uncle Wit said rudely.

"Well, not exactly. I heard you tell Carrie that she should just try new things and move on if it's not for her. I find that an extremely poor decision-making model. I know praying and seeking the Lord about something is always better. You can skip much of the trial and error by trusting God. I think that's all Carrie was trying to say," the pastor said.

"Maybe you're right, pastor, and maybe you're not," Uncle Wit said calmly. He offered the pastor the continuation of the view.

"One last thing and I'll leave you be. We talked earlier, before the ride, and you acted just fine towards me. When I told you I was a pastor, you threw up every defense you had. There's a word for that—anxiety. I appreciate your time," the pastor said with Godly authority. It set Uncle Wit aback.

After thirty minutes of drifting, Carrie seemed content and worry free. She knew she and the pastor had said enough to Uncle Wit. *He can chew on that for a while,* she thought. *I hope he chokes on it.* Her hair was still blowing in the breeze, and her hands were relaxed on the side of the gondola's rim. She continued looking forward and pondering her future and what Uncle Wit had said. She was quietly thanking God for the beauty and majesty. The offer from Zeb also came to mind, and for a moment, she did wonder what her ancestors might have done, and if she was from tangled roots?

"I'm glad you rode with me today, Carrie. It's been fun so far," Uncle Wit said boldly. Carrie knew it was a cover for his uneasiness.

"Yeah, I'll remember this for a long time. I was scared at first, but I'm glad I did it. The more I think about it, though, I think I should've asked Mom, so—" she stopped talking as the balloon suddenly lurched and ascended rapidly.

"Hold on, everybody! Wow, that's a strong updraft!" Troy said with emotion. "All the black summer fallow is heating things up."

Seeing that Troy was busy, Uncle Wit took over the explanation for the pilot. "That black soil down there absorbs the sun's heat and causes the air to warm and rise. It's a big area of crop rotation."

"Well, I don't want to go higher," Carrie quickly said.

Uncle Wit ignored her and continued, "It's where they let the land rest for a year, so there's no crop on it. Looks like some corn stubble is on it, though, from last year. We're just feeling the effect of that, Carrie. No worries."

Carrie was now hanging on to the side of the gondola with a white-knuckled grip. The sudden rise in altitude was a bit quick for her stomach. She felt sick. "When do you think we'll land, Troy?" she asked in a shaky voice.

"I'm pulling on the parachute valve now, honey. I'm ready to start descending, just as soon as we clear this updraft. It's a strong one," Troy said with a strange grunt in his voice.

As suddenly as before, the balloon listed sideways and began descending rapidly. It was like a downhill rollercoaster at the amusement park, but the hill didn't end. Released from the rising air, the balloon caught the falling cooling air and began losing altitude quickly. Carrie could see Troy watching the altimeter out of the corner of his eye.

"We're falling at 800 feet per minute. I want you all to sit on the floor and hold on for a minute or two. It could be a bumpy ride," Troy demanded.

"Is that too fast, Uncle Wit?" Carrie asked.

"Carrie, everything will be okay," he answered.

"I know that the average descent is 400-600 feet per minute, so that's a lot!" said the pastor. "I read all about these things before the trip up here," he added.

"Wouldn't hurt to pray now, would it, pastor?" Uncle Wit said rather disrespectfully.

A loud rush of gas came from the burners as Troy attempted to slow the descent by heating the air. He held the burners on for what seemed like an eternity. "You must have eaten an extra biscuit, Wit," he said to lighten to mood. Nobody laughed. "I have to put her down right here, folks. We were only 1650 feet up when we hit that updraft, and that's why it felt so strong. We got on the back side of that draft and into the falling cold air. We were falling too fast, but I don't want to shoot past Lewis. This is the safest place to set down, so hold on; we're moving at a good clip now," Troy said.

As the cooler air pushed closer and closer to the ground it billowed out in all directions. Half of it found its way back into the updraft, but the other half whirled out and away. The balloon followed this course, too.

"We could upset the basket," Uncle Wit said. "So, hold on!"

"When we get close to the ground, Wit, throw out that cooler and lunch kit and my stool," Troy ordered. "I don't want it hitting anybody."

Uncle Wit stood up and waited as the ground came up quickly. He took hold of the cooler and the lunch kit and readied for his throw. Carrie reached for the stool from her seated position and slid it over toward Uncle Wit. The pastor held two other ladies in his arms as they readied for the landing.

"Now!" Troy yelled.

Uncle Wit threw it all overboard as directed, and the pilot pulled the gas lever again and again. Carrie could hear the brush and small branches scraping under the gondola which gave a good indication of the rapid speed they were traveling.

Boom! Uncle Wit went sailing up and over Carrie but caught the side of her cheek with his knee as he did. He had been ejected out of the basket as the bottom hit the ground and then slid nearly on its side for 200 feet or more. Carrie and the other passengers were on the down side of the gondola when it hit, and they were safely riding it out sitting with their knees pulled in and on their backs. Pulling hard on the parachute valve rope, Troy found himself standing on the rim of the gondola hanging on to the burner frame. The basket didn't correct itself when it stopped. Small twigs and brush caught the hair of one lady and the pastor's hand was scraped by stiff branches and weeds as they made their way into the gondola. Eventually, everybody managed to climb out on their hands and knees, but stood up quickly due to the thick brush they were in. The envelope was wagging in the wind, and a few ripping sounds could be heard as the wind pulled it this way and that.

"Uncle Wit, Uncle Wit! Are you okay? Uncle Wit!" Carrie screamed. There was no answer.

"I see him!" said the pastor. "Let's go!"

The pastor and Carrie ran down to Uncle Wit as the balloon had come to rest on the side of a brushy hill. Uncle Wit lay nearly 200 feet downhill from where they stopped face down in the weeds.

The pastor and Carrie arrived quickly. "Uncle Wit, can you talk, can you move, Uncle Wit?" Carrie yelled. She was afraid to touch him but laid her hand on his back caringly. He moved a little and turned his head toward her and the pastor.

"What's that line in your poem about atoning? Well, I'm sorry for sure now," he said with effort.

"No time for jokes, mister. If you're okay, Wit, I'll let you stand up on your own. Think you can do that?" asked the pastor.

"Maybe. I jarred my back, just a little sore on my backside; I can try to get up," he said.

He rolled over and moaned a bit while Carrie and the pastor hoisted him off the ground and onto his feet. It was a difficult walk uphill through the brush; they found Troy and the others unharmed. Troy and the ladies were all trying to keep the balloon envelope up and off the brush as they gathered it into a ball.

The pastor outstretched his hands and requested the attention of everybody for a moment. "I want to say a few words here before the chasers arrive and take this opportunity to remind us all that God is protecting us. We owe Him a lot for this one. Mr. Wit, I don't usually do this sort of thing outside of my church family, and I would never wish to embarrass anyone, but I have to share what the Holy Spirit is impressing upon me. . .I don't know you, but look around. We're in the middle of nowhere, and God wants us to know that He has placed us together for a purpose. Please don't lose sight of that, and for the rest of us, let's thank God we're all just fine."

With that, the pastor began to pray but was interrupted by Uncle Wit, "I don't even know your name, Mister. Tell us all your name."

"You're right, I'm so sorry. Thank you, Wit. My name is Dakota Red Leaf. I'm the pastor of Omaha Word and Fellowship. These are my two sisters, Kimimela and Macha," he said, "and I would like to pray with you all right now."

"Wait. . .I would like to know about the purpose of all this, Mr. Dakota. I'm not sure what you mean about me losing sight of it," Uncle Wit said in an irritated way.

"You can look at her. . .your niece. If you don't know what the Lord is speaking to you about by now, I suggest you look this sweet little thing in the face and tell her yourself. I don't know how you could ignore her when she was trying her best to share the Lord's good news with you up there," Pastor Red Leaf said with great authority and ended the debate.

Uncle Wit's head hung, indicating a loss of control over the situation, and it readied him for prayer. Carrie knew by the name Red Leaf that he was of Lakota ancestry. She also knew the reputation of the Lakota people as strong and determined, and she knew Uncle Wit understood that as well. With such great leaders as Sitting Bull and Crazy Horse in the Lakota ranks, it was easy for Carrie and her uncle to assume, he too, had come from tangled roots. Carrie remembered reading about the Lewis and Clark Expedition in the early 1800s and how the Lakota controlled the Missouri River. After one parlay and overnight stay, the Lakota demanded twisted tobacco carrots before the expedition was released from their grips. Carrie and Wit knew he was "a force to be reckoned with," especially with God on his side.

Pastor Red Leaf began his prayer, "*Dear God of our universe, we come to you on this hillside to bless your name and proclaim your glory. We have just witnessed your protecting hand and mercy for our lives. It is a beautiful day and we are blessed enjoying it. Help us, Father, to understand why we are placed here together. Help us leave here knowing more about your ways and our own directions. Thank you for a safe landing and go with us as we contemplate what we have experienced today."*

It was a touching moment as everybody called out, "Amen!" Carrie was staring at Uncle Wit and noticed a slight tear in his eye as Pastor Red Leaf ended. "Uncle Wit, we better call Zeb and let him know where we are," Carrie said.

Carrie reached for her back pocket to retrieve her phone but remembered she had left it in the car because she had no back pockets. To her astonishment, she pulled out her car keys from her right front pocket.

"Oh, no!" she called out. "Zeb couldn't chase us; I have the car keys. This is terrible," Carrie cried as she sat down in the dirt in disbelief. "Where is he? What have I done?"

"The other chasers are pulling up. See, look to the north. See the highway? That's them," Uncle Wit comforted.

He was pointing north across a seemingly endless field of short brush and tumble weeds. The ground was rough and unused. In the distance, a small rise of earth formed what Uncle Wit was calling the highway. It seemed so far away; probably a mile or so by Troy's estimate. Carrie began to cry and placed her head on Uncle Wit's chest.

"Don't you get it? I left him stranded back there. All because I was trying to be an adult and make my own decision. I'm terrible at this. Zeb and Mom are gonna be so mad. . .I'm dead," Carrie cried.

"I'll take up for you, Carrie," Uncle Wit assured.

"Are you kidding me?" She looked up at him. "My mother is probably going to euthanize you at the clinic. You'll never be able to see me again. And I had fun with you today. Every time we get together something exciting happens, but this is too much for Mom. She's going to blow a head gasket!" Carrie exclaimed.

"You all get going, I'll wait here for the team to arrive; the envelope is all but wrapped up. Thanks, ladies," Troy groaned as he lifted the gondola basket into a precarious upright position.

CHAPTER 5

Peace

They began walking toward the distant highway, stepping around and over the wild growth of brush and small melon-sized rocks. It wasn't long before Carrie could make out the type of vehicles parked along the road and saw people climbing over the barbed wire fence that lined it. One vehicle was a large white van with writing on the side. It looked familiar to her as she drew closer. Still nearly 200 yards from the road, her face dropped, and she pushed Uncle Wit in front of her.

"What are you doing, you crazy kid?" he asked.

"That's Mom and Dad's van from the clinic," she said.

"Oh, you're in trouble now." He laughed uneasily.

"Please, stop! What do I say to her, Uncle Wit?"

"Just tell her you were trying to be an adult and make some decisions for yourself. Then tell her you learned a lesson. She'll appreciate your honesty. Then, I'll butt in, and she'll start on me. So don't worry," he quipped. "I've got your back."

Tripping several times, Carrie's mother tried to make her way toward the group in the open field but gave up. She didn't get far from the fence. By this time, Carrie had gathered up enough nerve to come out from behind Uncle Wit. She had scampered off ahead of him in an effort to circumvent the inevitable fight of the century. "Mother," she called. The two found themselves in an awkward embrace. The look on her mother's face was of concern, and Carrie was uncertain what was coming next.

"Your face! Look at your cheek!" her mother cried loudly and with great concern. Carrie knew her mother's technique well—the designation of blame with obvious overreactions and drama intended for others to hear. "What happened to it? Carrie, it's all bruised and turning really dark. Does it hurt?"

"No, Mom. It happened in the landing; I just bumped it. It will be okay, Mom," Carrie said.

"Well, you have a good friend in Zeb, that's all I can say," her voice was slowly raising in pitch as she spoke. "If it weren't for him, you'd be walking home for sure. I just wish you would think about what you are doing before you take a notion and do it. You're so immature!" her mother shrieked.

"Mom, there are other people here. Please let's talk at home, okay?" Carrie asked.

"Ma'am, can I have a word with you?" Pastor Red Leaf approached Carrie's mom.

Pastor Red Leaf talked with her for several minutes, but Carrie couldn't make out what was being said. He had pulled her away from the group and spoke in low tones. Eventually, she rejoined Carrie, and Pastor Red Leaf headed for the fence.

The chase-team with the trailer had parked on the side of the road and was unloading the four-wheeler to retrieve the balloon. Others were helping the pastor and the two ladies negotiate the barbed wire fence. Having no entrance for the four-wheeler close by, Uncle Wit was directing members of the team farther east where he had seen the end of the fence from the air. A small dirt road wound its way around the other side of the hill and would serve them perfectly. The team pulled a small two-wheeled trailer behind the four-wheeler just big enough for the gondola with the envelope tucked down inside. Uncle Wit hopped over the barbed wire and jumped on the tiny trailer dragging his feet in the dirt as they drove way.

"Just a minute, Wit. I want to talk to you!" Carrie's mother called out. But, she was too late. The noise from the motor drowned her out, and Uncle Wit just waved at her with a quirky smile. It made Carrie laugh. She quickly came to her senses as her mother pulled her arm and turned toward the van. Carrie then realized that Uncle Wit was avoiding his promise to have her back. Or was he? Carrie decided he was wanting her to be the adult in the situation. She quickly shed that thought and resolved within herself that she would retaliate. Carrie recalled the boys in her gym class and thought how immature and similar they were to Uncle Wit. Surely, she could deal with her mother alone. "I got your back," she quietly muttered. "Yeah, right!"

Carrie's mother walked with quick and angry movements. Carrie could tell her mother wanted answers.

"I want to know how this balloon ride got started. Zeb was very careful what he said to me. I could tell he was covering up for someone here!" her mother said accusingly.

"It's all on me, Mom, all on me. Let's go home; I'll talk in the car," Carrie moaned.

Chase-team members helped them duck through the barbed wire fence. One team member tried to assess the bruise on Carrie's cheek, but she reassured them of its insignificance, then jumped into the van. The ride home was therapeutic for Carrie and her mother. Carrie decided to change the subject to eliminate the lecture about Uncle Wit and the balloon ride. It worked perfectly, but at a cost. Carrie had to finally speak about the job incident and how embarrassed she was, crying about the lost ice cream and acting so immaturely. The decisions she'd made were not so bad; it was the "thinking things through" part that needed work. They both laughed about Zeb's predicament when he found no keys for the car. Her mother told her that Zeb had not wanted to make the call, but felt he had no choice, because the other chase-team members had already left by the time he arrived at the car.

"What did he say, Mom?" Carrie asked with her hands raised to her cheeks afraid to hear it.

"He said, 'Carla, your daughter got the trip of her life today. She got to ride in a hot air balloon.' So, I said, Oh, well that's nice. Did she have fun?"

"Is that it?" Carrie asked.

"Oh, no. I then asked where you were. That's when he told me you were still in the balloon headed to Lewis, and he had no way of following," her mother said. "When I asked who you were with, he hesitated. I knew then that something was up. He then told me you were with Wit."

"Were you mad, Mom?" Carrie asked.

"No, not really. I had just about gotten over this thing with Wit. Especially since you feel so strongly about him. I read your paper the other night, Sweetheart, and I saw things from another viewpoint. It crushed me, but I'm better now," her mother said.

"Mom, I had no idea. You read my report about Uncle Wit? Oh, no. I made up a bunch of that stuff just for the grade, Mom. A lot of it wasn't even true. I'm so sorry, Mom. Really. . .a lot of it wasn't even true!" Carrie stammered.

"It's okay, even if half of it is true, I know how you feel about him; I wasn't going to yell at him today, ya know. I was going to thank him for watching over you, because I know with every weird thing he does, he loves you. . .and me, and would never hurt either of us. His ways are unexplainable and unpredictable; he just has his own way of thinking. . .I guess," her mother said. "Pastor Red Leaf shared with me his burden for Wit. He said he had never met him before but felt so strongly about him. He told me how strong you were and how you stood up for your beliefs. He told me he was very impressed with you, Carrie. He wants us to pray for Wit and help him find direction in his life. I feel very bad, Carrie. A stranger had to tell me this, and Zeb tried, too. All these years I wanted to hate him, yet today, last night, the night before. . .it all makes sense, babe," her mother said, and rather slowly she ended, "The Lord works in mysterious ways."

CHAPTER 6

A New Effort

Despite her track record, Carrie continued her adult decision-making efforts. She didn't want to continue tearing herself down. "Everyone makes mistakes," she continually reminded herself. She would never forget about the lessons learned thus far. Even so, she agonized over the fact that everything she decided to do filtered through thoughts of maturation, endlessly running through the gauntlet of persuasion and doubt. The blows came from both sides of her conscience, like the iconic depiction of the angel and devil's shoulder perch—the symbolic battle of good and evil imagery. She wanted to leave her reactive reality for an active one—one where she responded with proper decision making skills. Worrying about every decision taxed her mind, but because she actually considered her decisions, a learning curve developed. Carrie had figured out the bad decisions affecting only her were not as big a mistake as the ones that affected others. She could now weigh this. "I can't just simply live and do like I did before," she often thought. But, she was much improved, and her outlook, together with her good decisions, were racking up in her favor.

Fall passed quickly, and Carrie decided not to worry too much about a job. Her church engaged her public speaking talents as narrator for the Christmas play, and she toured with the choir during the Thanksgiving and Christmas season to various venues. School was also an issue as the college entrance exam classes were offered, which she believed to be fairly important. Carrie took every practice exam she could find online and ordered a paper study copy as well. Debate and conversation came easy to her but not general scholastics, although, history would never fail her. She was disappointed that there was not more history on the college entrance exams; the Math and English topics were not her favorites.

Winter seemed long and boring with many cold nights locked in her room with books and homework. Friends didn't call frequently enough, and Zeb hadn't graced her doorstep in weeks. His girlfriend was back, and his time with her was important to him. Through it all, she kept her promise to herself and weighed the consequences carefully before acting. It worked, and she rode through winter with very few negative interactions with her mother. However, Uncle Wit nearly ran half the family off at Christmas dinner after bringing a large ham. He had stored it in his refrigerator for weeks, and when Carla unwrapped it in the kitchen, she and others nearly died from the smell of rot. He apologized and quickly ran out for another. Carla held her anger but still used the event to berate him without mercy, drawing parallels to his perpetually stagnant life. It was extremely harsh in Carrie's mind. Gifted in the art of communication, she understood the weight of the attack. Fortunately, Uncle Wit didn't hear it personally from her lips, but gathered up little pieces from other family members upon his return, enough to confront her, but he decided not to do for Carrie's sake. The comments wounded Carrie just as much as her mother's refusal of apology, even after several promptings. Carrie didn't forget her mother's choice easily, and she questioned her mother's sincerity about wanting to help Uncle Wit.

Spring came early to Council Bluffs. There hadn't been a lot of snow over the winter. Carrie could feel the need to get out and enjoy some evenings with her friends. She had decided that she was in control during the girls' nights out, and compromise of right choices would not be part of her life when these choices were made. Most of her friends respected that; however, a few nights ended with quarreling and tears, or simply disappointment in the expectations for some. During these times, Carrie simply considered these her adult decision-making experiences.

And as always, she was tested once again as three girls from her high school arrived in her driveway honking the horn on a warm spring Saturday evening. One of the girls was riding in the bed of an old red Subaru Brat, a small two-door miniature pickup, with bucket seats and handles mounted to the frame in the box of the vehicle. They waved and screamed Carrie's name so loudly several neighborhood lights flickered on. Carrie looked out of the front door and screamed, too.

"What are you doing, you crazy people?" she screamed as she ran towards the driveway.

The girls giggled and talked for some time before the difficult question came. And as it had so many times before, that statement on the poster, which was now hanging on the wall behind the bathroom door, made its appearance in her mind. Visible behind her from the mirror, that poster reminded her each morning what she would need to do. She wanted the poster's words to be backwards like she had first read it. It made a big impression on her, and each morning as she combed, curled, or crimped her hair, she worked out the words slowly as she had so many times before. The most difficult decision you will ever have to make.

"Jump in the back, Carrie," the young driver said. "We'll cruise for a while. Keggy and the gang are down at Merk's Diner."

"Wow, that sounds great, Zoe, but Mom and I are enjoying a TV show right now. Maybe next time," Carrie said.

Groans and "ahhhs" came from the girls along with more insistence that she go. One girl reminded her of her nickname, No-No, but she didn't yield to the pressure. Her mother, standing in the doorway just out of sight, listened to what was being said. Her hands were wringing together in a tight grip that seemed anxious, but Carrie eased her pressure as she cleared the threshold and closed the wooden door tightly and locked it. "Let's get back to it," Carrie said.

"Carrie, that was so mature of you, and nice," her mother said.

"Okay, Mom, I don't need to be told every time I amaze you. I just didn't want to miss my show, that's all," Carrie said. But she did need to hear it, and she gave some good thought to the moment; she would think this one through and milk it for all it was worth, even if it might not be the exact truth.

She let a moment pass and began to laugh. "I got you, Mom. I'm just kidding. I wanted to spend my time with you, old lady, now hit play," she said.

That night, Carrie continued to appreciate the compliment. She lost herself in her bathroom mirror while brushing her teeth and hair. There were several other times that her mother had noticed her adult assertiveness. She remembered back a few weeks when her brother had pitched a temper tantrum in a toy store over a wanted action figure. Several people had walked by glaring at them. Carrie took him by the hand with the action figure, laid it on the front counter, and walked out of the store. Her brother still in tow, and her mother following a bit behind, she stopped at the corner in front of a poor man with a sign. In front of her little brother, she asked the man how much it would cost for a nice meal and a warm cup of coffee. The man stated that twenty dollars would suffice. Without time for processing to take place in Pete's mind, Carrie asked him if he could, in good conscience, buy the action figure knowing the man was hungry. Pete shook his head and began to cry and apologized to his mother and ran to her arms. Her mother had only five dollars left in her purse but handed it to Pete. He took one step closer and handed it to the poor man. No more was said, but a smile lit her mother's face that could be seen from outer space.

Thrust back into reality, and realizing the time, Carrie began brushing her hair more quickly, but something didn't seem right. The door was open to the bathroom, and it obscured the poster behind her. Requiring the poster for her nightly routine, she grabbed the door and tried to shut it. Her brother appeared and ran quickly behind her.

"Carrie, what does that poster mean?" he asked. "I can't read it very well."

She closed the door enough to see the poster. "Try it in the mirror, Pete," she said. "Start from the right side though."

"It's backward, Carrie," he said.

"I know, Pete, but that's how I first read it. Give it a try," his sister said.

Pete called out what he could, "the. . ..mosted. . .biffi. . ."

"The mosted biffi, what does that mean, Pete?" she said, laughing.

They laughed together for a short bit. But Carrie kneeled and closed the door all the way. She held him by the shoulders closely and laid her cheek on the side of his arm. She read the words slowly and deliberately to him, "The most difficult decision you will ever have to make."

"What decision is it talking about?" Pete asked.

"You see that old dog in the picture? That's the best friend that man has ever had. He would never want his friend to suffer, so he's talking to the lady about helping his dog," Carrie said.

"Ooh," Pete said, "that's what Mom and Dad do at work. . . use-tin-A-ja, I think."

"That's right, euthanasia; you're a smart boy. I'm just glad that dog in the picture was still healthy, and he went home that day. Aren't you glad, Pete?"

"Yeah," he said as he opened the door and bolted down the hall and around their father, who had been listening to them through the door.

"Carrie, that was a beautiful thing you did for your brother. You really softened the blow of reality of that picture for him. I know you love your brother," her father said.

"Thank you, Dad, I just don't want him being reminded of death when he sees that picture. I don't want him to worry about that stuff," Carrie said.

"Do you worry about it? Why is that poster even here? I had it in the clinic," he said.

"No, Dad! I like the phrase. It reminds me to do the right thing. . .somehow, so I wanted it here, that's all," Carrie said.

"I love you, Sweetheart; you're a good big sister and a great daughter. Now, get yourself to bed before I throw you in the kennel," he said, laughing. "And Carrie, I hope you know that I'm here if you ever want to talk about adult things. If something is bothering you, I want you to know I'll take time for you."

"I know you would, Dad. My only worry at the moment is finding a job. So go to bed and say your prayers, for me," she laughed.

Time had gotten away from her during the past months. It was time to set her mind on securing a job for the summer. She knew she had the ability to find one, but she could not skip school to do it. At school during her study hall, she used the phone in her counselor's office to call prospective job opportunities. Graduation was just a couple months away, and Carrie was feeling the pressure. A friend had questioned her rather rudely about not knowing where or what she would do for the summer, but her future and career didn't come up, surprisingly. *Probably because Wendy doesn't know what she wants to do either,* she thought. But it was no consolation, and she began to discredit herself again. It took Zeb a week to talk her out of the reactive reality she let others create for her, and by the following week, job hunting continued. She didn't reach out to retail stores this time. She focused on the service industry: delivery, cleaning, even shelf stocking and warehouse jobs. Carrie was able to secure two job interviews on Saturday before noon. The first interview would be with a man from a seed company. The second was at a new kind of nursing home called an adult daycare where the residents went home at night.

Saturday morning arrived, and Carrie had almost finished preparing her small purse on the kitchen counter when the phone rang. "Wish me luck, Mom. I'm going to my interviews, you'll have to get the phone. Tell Dad, too, will ya," Carrie yelled again, running out the back door.

"Why don't you pray about it?" her mother yelled back.

"Good idea, I will," was all her mother heard before she disappeared. Carla answered the phone.

Running to the car, Carrie wondered who had called, but left the thought and took her mother's suggestion of prayer. A prayer was said in the car, and afterward, Carrie felt a little guilty over the avidness of it. She didn't want to sound pretentious, but she wanted to believe that God was watching her and would help. Zeb had reminded her that when God sees the action and intention to carry out His will, and the desire to be in His will, blessings flow. "All for His glory," Zeb would say. The words calmed her, and the thought of herself being a blessing felt good.

She arrived early to her first appointment, so the man at the seed company readied himself and showed Carrie around the yard. Men and women were bagging grass and wheat seed, filling buckets with corn, soybeans, and sunflower seeds, and one building was dedicated to bagging bird seed. It was dusty and dirty work—not like what she had pictured. It didn't look overly complicated. *I'm definitely overqualified,* she thought, and the dust was more than she wanted to deal with.

Carrie was not shy, and before long, she had come to her senses about the tour. "Sir," she said, "I'm sorry for taking your time today, but I think I'll have quite a time with my allergies with a job like this. I didn't imagine the dust, and I don't think I'll be able to handle it. But, thank you so much for the time you took showing me around."

"That's fine. This is why I always start out here even before we talk. I get that a lot. I don't like it, either," he said with a laugh. "But, I'm not looking for a worker out here. I need a cleaner for the seed gravity separators and the room they're in. It's not so dirty in there." They walked for a time to a large tall building called a grain elevator which was across the street from the bagging company.

After entering the office side door of the grain elevator, the man explained, "These machines take in samples of farmers' grains and count the number of weed seeds and other undesirables in a crop, they're called shaker tables, and then we test for the grain's moisture. We've got to give the farmer a fair price. This room opens up to the shoots, where we receive the grain from the farmers' trucks, and it gets a little dirtier than the next rooms. Come through here, and I'll show you where I need some help. I like it clean in here because we sell planting seeds to farmers; every seed counts in here." They walked through a long corridor to a large back room. "These are called gravity separators," he explained.

The room was filled with large machines with shaking platforms, large hoppers and overhead spouts and transfer tubes. The machines blew air from the underside up through a large plate onto which seeds dropped and danced across, being separated by vibration and air flow. It was a marvelous sight, and the seeds and debris miraculously separated and moved in different directions. Each machine had an operator, and each machine managed a different seed. It was much cleaner than the other sites.

"I see. I was imagining cleaning the old-fashioned way with rags and buckets," she said with a laugh, "but you mean cleaning seeds—Aaahhh!" Carrie screamed. "A mouse!"

Carrie ran towards the man and stood behind him. She was dancing a little jig and moving her body in a frightened way. The man began to laugh at her, as well as the other two men in the room.

"Mice are always around a grain elevator, Carrie. Aw, it's just a little guy," the man said.

"My pa had one run up his leg at his animal clinic. I'll never forget that! I'm very afraid of them," Carrie cried.

"Well, dust and mice aren't for you, I guess. We can't get rid of mice; we can only control the numbers," he said. "It was nice to meet you, Carrie. Come on through this door, and I'll walk you to your car." They walked across the street, laughing. The man made her feel at ease about the whole thing. He told her about his granddaughter who acted the same way when seeing a mouse. He mentioned how she had to sit in the movie theater with her feet on the chair for fear of mice running up her pant leg. Carrie laughed with him but realized that she did the same thing in a theater. She didn't share that. They made their cordial goodbyes, and Carrie sighed heavily as she pulled onto the road. "What was I thinking?" she said quietly to herself.

Carrie had some free time before her next interview at the adult daycare. She decided to stop by her parents' animal clinic, even though she hated the place. She secretly wanted a little insight from her father on the adult daycare she was about to visit. However, he offered her a job at the clinic that paid real money, just as much as the other workers received when they started. Her father had offered her a job many times, but she didn't want to be there any more than she had to. Occasionally, she did volunteer there, but it was out of guilt, and that was hard enough on her. She hated to see animals die. Many of the animals that came to the clinic were wild, so they were quickly transferred to the state agencies if they were well enough to be transported, and then eventually returned to their natural habitats. The others were euthanized. Some injured dogs and cats from the community saw a veterinarian first before arriving at the clinic. These were the ones with a chance for adoption. Her father fixed up the animals with minor issues. Many were placed with new families, but only two weeks were allotted for adoption, and so many were "put to sleep," as Carrie liked to call it. Her father teased and told her that the elderly people would all be adopted by the end of each day. She knew they were picked up by loved ones. "Very funny, Dad. When you get old, I'm leaving you there," she said in jest.

Carrie gleaned as much as she could from her father, then arrived right on time for her interview. She parked in the front circle of a beautiful yellow brick building with brown columns on either side of the entrance. There were large windows that looked out on all sides. It was a sunny and happy looking place. As she stood waiting for someonc to "buzz" her in, she wondered if she would be shown around first or just asked a lot of questions. A loud buzzer primed her focus as she walked in and was greeted by a door guard. He asked her to sign in and told her to have a seat. She was not nervous. . .until it was her turn. She was taken to a large day room by the front guard; a table and a few chairs had been set up near the center. She sat at the far end of the table and waited until three middle-aged people walked in, each shook her hand with a smile. They asked no questions, and after the brief introductions, the three-person panel described the interview process. The owner had to see if potential employees had the wherewithal to engage the clients in conversation. She was asked to speak for five minutes, which included explaining why she wanted to work there, what she loved, who she was, and anything else she felt was important enough to share. A timer set for five minutes was given to her. "Do not waste time," one of the individuals said.

Carrie had no time to think—no warning, no topic. She remembered what Zeb told her about car rides and talking. She quickly looked out the large picture windows and imagined herself in a car watching the trees go by.

"Well, hi there. My name is Carrie Barclay, and I would love to work with the folks here. I was born and raised right here in Council Bluffs. My favorite place to go is Sergeant Floyd Monument, along the interstate some miles north of here. I love to feel the wind in my hair on a warm summer day and see out across the valley where Meriwether Lewis and William Clark, and the whole Corps of Discovery once stood. Do you know who they are? They explored the Louisiana Purchase in 1803, and Sergeant Floyd was the only death they had on the two and a half year trip. . ."

Somehow Carrie stumbled into a 4-H speech about famous Americans she had given in the past, and she rambled on about other historical landmarks in the area as well. After three minutes, one of the panel members interrupted her and said, "Welcome to the team, Carrie; we believe you could talk for an hour like that. These old folks will just love to talk about that stuff. Can you start Monday night?"

"I sure can!" she said excitedly.

The panel congratulated her and took her to the game room where several elderly sat looking out the windows. "You'll work in this room with Edd, Berdella, and Wilma. Wilma is not here today, but you'll love her," a panel member said. "We'll see you Monday, Thursday, and Friday nights at 3:00 if that's good for you, and you will see these late ones out by 9:00 p.m. We don't want our residents just sitting like this; we want them engaged in meaningful conversation. We think you are perfect for that. You can go with Kate and fill out your papers. Congratulations."

Carried agreed and smiled the whole way back to the office. She left the facility on a cloud of air, and each step seemed as graceful as Fred Astaire. *Wow, Zeb is gonna love this,* she thought. *I found a job on my own merit, and my crazy talk got me the job.*

Zeb did enjoy it. Sunday after church, he laughed so hard with Carrie over the ordeal that Coke came out his nose while sitting in the local Burger Hut. "Boy, I wish I could have seen the looks on those people's faces. I bet they thought you would say a few words and then they would have to prompt you again, and again, and again. No way, not Carrie Barclay. If you pictured yourself in a car, no wonder you never shut up. Now they know how I feel riding with you." He kept laughing. "Did you get that crazy look in your eye, too, like you're hypnotized?"

"Laugh all you want, but I got a job on my own merit. . .and mouth. Maybe I'll own the place one day," she said, smirking.

CHAPTER 7

A Cold Apology

Carrie's family, the girls at school, Zeb, and Uncle Wit all heard about Carrie's great speech at the daycare facility and were all proud of her; all but a few of her friends who wanted nothing to do with the elderly. Carrie quickly reminded them of the security in it since there would always be old folks for which to care. Beth cheered her on and had occasionally accompanied Carrie to work.

One girl, who Carrie considered one of the "Mean Girls," just like in the movie, teased her about her new job. She continued to keep her close and laugh along as she teased, but it infuriated Carrie deep within. Her mother always told her to keep her friends close and her enemies closer. Zoe may not have been an enemy in the harshest definition, but Car rie felt no supportiveness from her.

"Can you change my diaper?" she would say with an old sounding frail voice. Often it was, "You goin' to the senior club tonight? You gonna hang out with your old friends, Carrie?"

Carrie confided in Beth and asked several times why an eighteen-year-old high school senior would want to act like that towards others. It was a bit confusing to Carrie since she thought she struggled with adult decisions. But, after two years of knowing her, Carrie finally learned the girl had no mother, and being raised by her dad, she probably acted out of insecurity. Finding her alone in the commons one day, Carrie approached her unafraid and with assertiveness.

"Zoe, can I talk with you for a minute?" Carrie asked

"Sure, Carrie, sit down. Waz up, girl?" Zoe asked.

"First of all, Zoe, I want you to know I'm not mad at you, so when you hear what I have to say, you'll know I'm not here to argue, okay?"

Zoe put her spoon down and sat up to listen. She looked rather intimidated by Carrie's opening, and it caught her off guard. "What did I do, Carrie?" she asked.

"Well. . .I'm very proud of my new job, the job I've been at now for a few months, but you're always teasing me about it, and I'm a little tired of being the butt of all your jokes. Just a few months ago you were at my house with the other girls wanting to ride to Merk's Diner and stuff. Are you mad that I didn't go with you that night? Was something said?" Carrie inquired.

"Carrie, Beth already said something to me about this, but I didn't pay much attention to her." She hung her head. "I really feel awful about it. I. . .I. . .," Zoe said as she began to cry. Her crying continued in silence for a few moments until Carrie laid her hand on top of hers. The touch was warm and caring, and it was not usually Carrie's way. She had her times of tenderness, but she was usually more direct and exacting in her tone, so it came as a surprise to Carrie just as much. Zoe left her seat and hugged Carrie just before leaving in a seemingly humiliated state. But several days later, Carrie received a note from Zoe via her other friends that cemented their friendship. Zoe had helped Carrie find a new way of communicating and dealing with adversity, and she took the lesson to heart, storing up the experience as a method for her inevitable confrontation she was preparing for with Uncle Wit.

After a few months on the job, Carrie had turned the heads of the staff. She was remarkable in her interactions with the residents at the facility, but it came with a cost. Carrie, so certain of her abilities in conversation, actually studied for her job. She spent homework time looking up topics to discuss with Edd and the others. She neglected her schooling at times and played catch-up with assignments; as a result, some of the families started requesting their loved one spend time with Carrie. She relished in the knowledge. The staff was overwhelmed with requests, and one panel member jokingly suggested a higher price be charged for time with Carrie. Moreover, Carrie jested a higher wage should be paid for the interest being generated. The three o'clock hour became a favorite time for the elderly and their families. It was the time she spent with Edd that developed the most interest. The other staff members brought their clients in to listen to the conversations about historical figures, Edd's war stories, the world news, and good jokes. Carrie would pose thought provoking topics to Edd, and he would respond with impeccable judgment on any of the issues. Carrie would play the Devil's advocate with him, and the debate would rage even after regular hours. Nobody wanted to leave. Edd was becoming dear to her, along with Wilma and Berdella. Wilma's laughter made everybody laugh, and her German accent was an endearing trait. Berdella was nearly deaf and would ask silly questions that were so far off topic Carrie could only respond with a hug. Her favorite time was the evening worship service and nightly prayer time. Carrie offered a short devotional reading and prayed for the residents before they left for the night. At this time, the room was usually packed with the adult children of many of the elderly, and word spread quickly about her.

Despite the wonderful work at the daycare, she missed her friends on those late spring evenings when the backyards of her friends became an impromptu gathering point. Sundays were nice since she would go to church early and see her best friends before Sunday school. Zeb was always there, too. After church, the group would enjoy a lunch at a popular fast food restaurant and laugh and giggle the entire time. She felt that quitting her job to spend time with friends was an immature thing to do, and she continued working at saving her money. "This is what adulthood looks like," she validated.

The money was great, and she had already earned enough to pay back Mr. Gibson at the ice cream store. She couldn't wait to do it. She knew he would find her mature and honorable. Her mother had suggested she garnish her own wages as discipline suggesting she would not miss it as badly. Zeb had already told her how mature that would be, so she really had no choice in the matter. She would never forget the regret she felt if she didn't make it right. In Sunday school, Carrie shared her plans with Zeb, and he rehearsed a few good lines to say to Mr. Gibson, including some absurd ones that made Carrie laugh. "Ask him if he has any CA-SHEEEEW Ice cream, or, 'Do you serve tissue with your ice cream?'" he joked. Zeb wished her luck and gave her a hug. Carrie was thankful for his help.

The big apology day arrived; it was a rainy gloomy day, a Monday no less. Carrie had completed her third quarter finals the Friday before and was out of school for the day. She could see Mr. Gibson during the daytime hours. Encouraged by the words on her poster, she beamed with confidence as she partially dried her hair, braided it to one side, dressed her best, and headed out the door to make her world right.

She parked her little silver Corolla and walked into the mall. She continued the long walk through a rather quiet indoor mall, listening to her feet squeak on the marble floor as she walked. Carrying a brown paper bag, she opened the door to Arley's Ice Cream and Cone. There on one of the blue benches he sat.

"Uncle Wit, what are you doing here?" she asked.

"Well, I'm eating ice cream, eating ice cream on a slow and rainy Monday. I'm off work today," he said.

"Ya know, every time I've seen you since the balloon ride there's always been so many people around. I wanted to talk to you about that trip. This is a good place and time, but give me just a minute," Carrie said.

Mr. Gibson came out of the back room with a handful of cones. "Well, look who it is," he said.

"Mr. Gibson, before you say anything, I just want to tell you how sorry I am for what happened a few months back. It was a terrible accident, and it was not very mature of me. I know it cost you money," Carrie said respectfully as she reached out her hand with ten twenty-dollar bills fanned out perfectly. "Here's the money I think will cover my mistake."

"Oh, no, Carrie. That's not necessary. I acted like a fool that day. I was just embarrassed in front of my customers, that's all. I covered that little thing." Mr. Gibson put down the cones and held his hand up in defense.

"You have to take this money. I want to pay you for the mistake. It's important that I do this, because I have to know I solved my own problems. I saved a long time for this, and I won't even miss it," Carrie pleaded.

"I'll take it," Uncle Wit called from his bench.

"You stay out of this, Uncle Wit," Carrie yelled back at him. She was standing in front of the Rocky Road ice cream bucket which was behind glass. "How much is that bucket of ice cream, Mr. Gibson?" she asked.

"Oh, I don't know. . .about eighty dollars or so, I guess. Why?" he asked.

"Well, I ruined two of those buckets, didn't I?"

"One was almost empty; you'll have to remember that. That's why you were so far down in the bucket." He laughed. "I'll tell you what. I'll take eighty dollars on your mistake if you promise to come and have ice cream with that man back there from time to time. You know, he's a mess," Mr. Gibson said, generating a laugh from both of them.

"He's my uncle; I guess you gathered that, and I think he's listening to our conversation," Carrie said.

"He's been a customer for years; never knew he had family around here," Mr. Gibson said, taking the money from Carrie.

"Okay, if that's what I have to do," Carrie said, "then eighty dollars will work for me. Thank you so much, Mr. Gibson." He turned and disappeared into the back room.

Uncle Wit made a motion to leave his seat. "Oh, no you don't. You'll stay right there, Mister. You and I are going to talk about something," Carrie said rather authoritatively. "I believed you after that balloon landing when you said you were going to have my back. Have my back, did ya? You left me with my mother when that was all your fault to begin with. You knew my mother would never have let me go up there without her," Carrie said.

"You didn't get it, did you?" he said. "I left the scene because it took the edge off of her anger towards you. When I left, she was free to be angry with me, and that would help you. I'm sure she threw me under the bus and blamed me for it all. That was your cue to pile on, too. Were you punished for it or not?" he asked

"Well. . .no. . .I guess not," Carrie answered.

"See, it worked. I had your back, and you didn't even get it. Now, Carrie, who's the smart one here?" Uncle Wit asked.

A long and awkward pause came between the two. "I am!" Carrie said with her shoulders pulled back. "That is a bunch of bologna, and you know it. You ran out on me because you were scared. You just sat there and made that up, right in front of me. That's your problem. You've always been scared to do the right thing, see things through, and do what's right. It's why you've drifted all these years. You can't commit. You need to decide—"

Carrie stopped, got very quiet, shifted her feet, and then sat down next to him calmly. The image of the poster came to her in a flash. She understood how important the phrase could be in a moment like this. She saw it clearly, and out it came. "Uncle Wit, you'll think this is the most difficult decision you will ever have to make, but it isn't. I want you to—"

Uncle Wit interrupted her obvious salvation message. He saw it in her sudden calmness, and he preempted it with shock and awe. "Your mother sent me over here to watch you apologize to Mr. Gibson."

"What!" Carrie said in absolute astonishment as she stood again.

It gave Uncle Wit his freedom, and he pressed around her and walked to the door. "I don't know; ask your crazy mother," he said.

"When did you talk to my mother?" She asked.

"Sunday night on the phone," he said as he opened the door and rounded the nearest corner.

Carrie stood in disbelief. *What is going on?* she thought. Resentment welled up in her as she reached for her cell phone. Now shaking as a result of her mother's apparent surreptitious operation, Carrie ran her finger through the cell phone list. She passed everybody's number and ended in the Zs. Zeb's number lit up her screen. She wanted to call her mother and ask her why she would try to embarrass her like that. *Why would she want Uncle Wit to watch me here?* she wondered.

Mr. Gibson came out from the back room just as two ladies entered the store. "Carrie, you okay there?" he asked. "Wait there, Carrie, I'll talk to you in a minute."

Carrie didn't have a minute. She left the seating area and sprinted out the door, but found herself walking aimlessly down one side of the strip mall and up the other side, twice, before walking to her car in the rain. Walking had a similar effect on her as did the car ride. She cleared her mind and determined to avert an argument when she got home. She knew she could not trust what Uncle Wit told her, but it made so much sense to her. Coincidence or not, she would play it cool and bounce questions off her mother to determine the truth.

In the car ride home she thought, and decided to bounce the whole story off of the seniors at the adult daycare. At least one of them was rational enough. Edd was a wise man, a lawyer for years and a school janitor for a few years in retirement, and he had heard all there was to hear. He told many funny stories and made everybody laugh. If anyone could make sense of this apparent betrayal by her mother, he could. Just recently he told her about the ballgames at the school and how the parents always made the players mad by yelling out their kids' names. She knew Edd had a special discernment. His children lived in distant places, and it was difficult for him; conversation with others eased his mind.

Carrie had a few hours before her shift started at the daycare center, so she completed some necessary homework assignments, but didn't see her mother as she readied herself for work. Her parents were not home from the clinic, but it didn't matter. Apprehension about an eventual discussion filled her mind, but she took solace in the knowledge of having Edd's point of view.

She walked into the daycare and greeted the door guard and the receptionist. As she turned to go down the hall, the director caught her by the arm.

"Hi, Carrie, could you help me with something real quick-like?" she asked.

She followed her into her office, and Kate sat down behind her desk. "Carrie, I have some terrible news for you. I'm so sorry, but Edd passed away early this morning in his bed. I'm so sorry, Carrie. He'll be so missed here," she said.

Carrie sat down in the side chair and began to cry. She sobbed inconsolably for a number of minutes before gaining any semblance of control. The director tried handing her tissues, but she wouldn't look up. Finally able to speak, Carrie asked, "When and where is the funeral, Kate?"

"Oh, Carrie, it's too early for that. We'll have to wait on the family," she said.

"Who told you he died?" Carrie asked.

"Well, A.J., our driver, was on his route to pick him up. Sometimes he liked to ride the transport, but he didn't come to the door. A.J. had a key and let himself in. He found him still in his bed. The E.M.T.s said it was likely a heart attack," Kate said.

The director left her chair and took a small box from the bookshelf. She then quietly closed the door and handed Carrie the small box wrapped in thick brown paper. "This is yours from Edd. He gave it to me only three days ago. There were strict orders placed on me to give it to you if he died. I argued with him about it, but he said for me not to worry and that he was not checking out any time soon, and he laughed. He told me he had been having some pain in his chest, so I reported it to his son in Fargo, and against his will, too," she said.

"What's in it?" Carrie asked.

"I don't know, but he said it was just a small trinket that meant something to him, and he wanted to show his appreciation for all the conversations with you. I think it might be a war medal or something like that. No matter what it is, it's yours now, so. . ."

"I understand; families can get real funny over stuff like this," Carrie said.

"Don't you want to open it?" Kate asked.

"No, not just yet," she said sadly.

Carrie did her best with the shift she had and with the other residents, and their families talked about Edd and shed their own tears. She helped them all make cards to deal with the grief. Carrie didn't discuss the little box wrapped in brown paper but tried changing the subject to her apology day at the ice cream store. Neither Berdella nor Wilma joined in the discussion. Everyone was gone by 9:00 p.m. It was a heavy night for all. She knew Thursday was three days away; the extra time would be needed to get over the shock. Carrie was exhausted, and all she could think about was sleeping under warm covers in her bed.

CHAPTER 8

Secrets and Trust

Morning came quickly, and she was awakened by her phone at 8:35 on a Tuesday morning. Her parents had already gone to work, and her little brother had been taken to school. Carrie didn't have class until 10:00 a.m. due to her work study rotation.

"Hello?" she said in a rather groggy voice.

"Carrie, this is your Uncle Wit. You awake, Carrie?" he asked in a rather short tone.

"Yeah, what's wrong, Uncle Wit? Are you okay?" Carrie asked.

"No, Carrie, I need your help real bad like. You've got to help, Carrie. I don't know what to do. I need to come get you. Are you dressed?"

"No, I'm not. You just woke me up. What's wrong with you?" she questioned with disdain.

"I'll be there in a few minutes, Carrie; get dressed, you've got to go with me!" he said quickly.

"I'm not going anywhere with you, Uncle Wit. Tell me what you need. I'm still mad at you," she said.

There was heavy breathing on the other end of the phone, and Carrie began to worry. She assumed he was being tracked by some mad men like in the movies and needed a get-a-way car or something.

"Are you in trouble Uncle Wit?" she asked. But before he could answer Carrie let loose of her problem from the night before. "I lost a dear friend yesterday, so I'm not in the mood for games. I need my sleep."

"Carrie, I'm driving now, and I'll be at your place in ten minutes. I don't have much time, so please just be ready to go." He disconnected the call, and Carrie sat up on the edge of her bed. She looked at the phone again to satisfy herself she didn't dream it. She sighed heavily and stood. Her bedroom mirror caught her reflection as she walked out of the room. "Yeah, you go that way, and I'll go this way. Maybe one of us is going in the right direction," she said aloud.

"Oh, so we meet again," she said as she looked at herself in the bathroom mirror. The poster loomed behind her with those backward letters. "I hope I'm doing the right thing here; what could this be about?" But she got no answers from her confused expression reflected in the mirror. "Okay, you go your way, and I'll go mine," she said as she finished her quick morning primp.

The doorbell rang before she could get down the stairs. It was Uncle Wit in a work uniform of some sort. He stood nervously with a Cammcore Plastics breast patch attached to his shirt; scrolled beneath it was his name.

"Are you ready?" he asked.

"Uncle Wit, you need to stop here for a moment and tell me what's going on," Carrie pleaded.

"Can I tell you in the truck?" he asked.

"Am I going to get into trouble for this? Is this going to get crazy? You're scaring me!" she exclaimed.

"Oh, Carrie, no, no, no, I just need help with something, that's all. Come on," he said rather calmly.

Carrie jumped into his old blue Ford truck and clicked her seatbelt. Uncle Wit began.

"Carrie, your mother and you. . .well, the whole family don't really know a lot about me. I guess you know me the best, so I feel like I can come to you for a little help. You're older now and will probably understand," he said.

"Spit it out, Uncle Wit," she said.

"Carrie, I got this new job after our balloon ride. The man driving that four-wheeler hired me that day. This morning he called me to his office and told me he was in trouble with the timing on a large bid and wanted me to get this paperwork to an office south of Council Bluffs. He asked me if I'd go, and I told him he could count on me. So, he handed me this here paper with the directions instead of a map," he said.

"You can't read?" she asked with great clarity and understanding.

"Aw, Carrie, it's not so much that. It all gets jumbled up with the numbers and things. I just can't process it right when I'm nervous and stuff," he responded.

"Do you have dyslexia?" Carrie asked.

"Yeah, something like that," Uncle Wit said. "But I have only a half hour to get this to the office where it needs to go. Can you help me? Please, Carrie," he pleaded. "I have to keep this job."

"Turn around, Uncle Wit. You're going east, and we have to go south on I-29, then catch I-80 into Omaha. This says it's in Nebraska. That's just over the river; it's near the zoo. Do you know where the zoo is over there?" she asked.

"Yes, I do, I used to work there," he said with a laugh.

"Well, go that direction. The address doesn't seem far from the zoo. This says turn on Bancroft Street. That's where Bancroft Elementary School is. I played basketball there years ago," she reminisced.

The truck cab was quiet as Uncle Wit headed down I-29 and merged unto I-80. Determination was etched in his face. He glared at his watch as he drove, counting every minute. He blew past the speed limit several times, but Carrie reminded him a ticket would take more time and probably cause him to fail on his mission.

"What's this bid for?" Carrie finally asked to help him forget the time.

"It's a $20,000 bid for these new plastic park benches we make. If I don't get this bid there in time, I'm done there for sure. I had an hour to do it, but I had to get you first. I think I lost too much time," he said worriedly.

"Oh, I know where this is. Lauritzen Gardens is a botanical garden park. Our school took a field trip there. We're close, Uncle Wit, very close. We'll have ten minutes to spare," she said.

"That's good to hear. Carrie, can you keep this between us? I mean the reading issue and things. I'm not sure your mother knows. I was quite a bit older, and I don't think she knows why I ran away from home. My folks didn't even know. Well, I mean, no one really knew why I had such troubles in school. I just found out when I applied for a job at the Red Cross. Those people pick up on everything. They really helped me a lot with stuff. When I was in school, there were the kids who could read and the kids who couldn't. I tried, and I can read a little; it just takes more time than I had today. You see don't you, Carrie?" he asked.

"Your secret is safe with me. But you should never have told me all that stuff about your tangled roots and trying new things when it doesn't work out or you don't like something. Now I know why Mom was so confused. A person should stick to something and work through it. You're trying hard to keep this job—why now?" Carrie asked.

"Oh, I didn't tell you anything that wasn't true about your roots. That's true; we all come from tangled roots. It's who we are. But, I don't have anything to show for my life because I didn't want help. It's very embarrassing. Your mother was right. She said my past ways of doing things have shown their compensation. That compensation is a big zero. I need a career, a retirement, and some good friends. I feel bad about talking to that pastor the way I did, and I feel bad about doing all that stuff to you and your mother. Carrie, there's something different about you. . .I trust you. You're a great niece," he said as they drove past the zoo.

"Just a few more blocks up this way." Carrie pointed. She wasn't trying to ignore the last statement, but she felt Uncle Wit was getting too introspective, and she was still a little upset with him. She wanted to empathize with him, but she would wait, as she would have a few minutes to think about it as he delivered the papers.

The old blue Ford stopped in front of a beautiful botanical garden. "Can you stay with the truck Carrie, and I'll run it in?"

"Yes, get going," Carrie encouraged.

Uncle Wit ran up the front walkway but stopped short of the door. He slowed to a calming steady walk and opened the door to a lovely space of beautiful colors and smells. At the front desk, a kind looking woman took his name and asked how she could help, but before he could answer, a woman dressed in business attire made her entrance through a door behind her.

"Ellen, have you heard from Cammcore Plastics? I'm expecting a bid on the new benches," she said.

Uncle Wit immediately spoke up, "Ma'am, I'm here from Cammcore Plastics, and I have that bid right here. I'm Wit Kline," he said.

"Well, great, you have impeccable timing, Mr. Kline," she said.

"Thank you for accepting our bid at such a late date. One of our suppliers took longer than usual getting back to us," Wit said.

"Our meeting starts in ten minutes, so we'll look at your products and proposal and get back to you sometime this week. Tell your boss 'thank you' from us," she said sweetly.

"Your name is. . .?" he asked.

"Oh, I'm sorry. My name is Laura Cloer," she replied as she shook his hand rather warmly. She placed her other hand on top of his for what appeared to be a deliberate delay.

Uncle Wit took the hint quickly and, without so much as a blink, replied, "The blue orchids by the door sure match the color in your eyes. They're lovely." He let her hand go slowly and turned for the door slowly. His eyes were set with confidence and pride.

"I'll be calling, now, Wit," she called to him as he lifted his hand in the air towards her.

Uncle Wit climbed back in the truck with wide eyes. He looked at Carrie and stared in silence. He finally heard her calling his name and answered. "Oh, sorry. . .You won't believe what just happened. Let's get out of here, and I'll tell you," he said.

Down the road a few blocks, Carrie couldn't wait to hear the news. "What happened in there, Uncle Wit?" she asked.

"That woman made a play for me. Well, I mean, showed interest in me," he said.

"What are you talking about? How do you know that?" Carrie said.

"Oh, I know. . .and I know we're getting that bid, too. Whoo hoo!" he hollered.

Uncle Wit was speeding again, and Carried scolded him. The ride became quiet again, but Uncle Wit seemed happy and was whistling as he drove past the zoo. "Look, there's Gee Gee the giraffe poking her head up. I used to feed her." He laughed; those were the days.

Carrie had her opportunity. While she waited in the truck for Uncle Wit earlier, she knew she had a captive audience in him for the ride home. She would witness to him one more time. "Lord, let him listen to me now," she prayed.

"Look at you, Uncle Wit, got the world by the tail. You can have anything you put your mind to I'll bet. Too bad you don't have the one thing, though," she said rather slowly.

"What's that, a girl?" he said.

"No, the Lord, Uncle Wit. Pastor Red Leaf was right. I see the Lord dealing with you right now. Just look at your newfound desire for this job. Where did that come from?" she said.

A soft rumbling of truck tires was all that could be heard for thirty seconds. Uncle Wit danced his fingers on the steering wheel but finally spoke, "You have impeccable timing. That's what the lady said to me. You have impeccable timing. . .so do you, Carrie. I knew this was coming, but I thought you were going to start in on me after that tangled roots comment," he said.

"Please just listen to me once. I have always tried to talk to you about stuff, but you're always so far away, even when you're right in front of me. Well, now we're alone, and you've told me some very private things. I know you're dealing with a lot of stuff, and so am I. My favorite senior at the daycare just died. I'm not sure how I'm going to deal with that, but I'm going to call on the Lord to help me. Why don't you do that with me?"

"Carrie, the Lord never helped me, no how. All my life, He never helped me. Why would He want to now?" he asked.

"You have it backwards, Uncle Wit. We were made with a choice, a choice to ask Him for His help. Have you ever, once, asked Him for help?" Carrie asked.

"No, no, I haven't, Carrie. Maybe that's on me, but the Bible was written by people long ago; what would they know about me, and what would I need with them? I'm a good guy. Sure I'm flawed, but I don't need to be saved. . .saved from what?"

Carrie's eyes began to moisten, and a tear ran down her cheek. Uncle Wit looked at her with surprise. It was evident he had not listened to her about last night. Her emotional state was badly weakened due to the death of Edd, and the Bible comment offended her, yet she stood her ground. "I'm going to tell you something that was told to me, and I know it's for you directly from the Lord. I was given this in Sunday school but didn't know who it was for, but it's clear now," she said with a crackle in her voice.

"Okay, Carrie, don't cry. I didn't mean to upset you," he said.

Carrie ignored his statement and continued, "C.S. Lewis, who was a Christian theologian, said, 'Until we rightly view our sinful state, we will never see our need for a Savior.'"

Uncle Wit looked her in the eyes for a lengthy amount of time. It made Carrie nervous, and she motioned for him to look at the road. The interstate was busy, and he would need to merge onto the off ramp shortly. She remained quiet so he could have the last word. Carrie would need to hear his next argument so she could develop a rebuttal. But there was no last argument. He focused on the road and said no more to Carrie until they returned home.

"Uncle Wit, I hope you have a good day. I'm glad I could help you. Don't worry about the reading thing. I won't say a word," she said.

"Okay, I really appreciate you carin' about me. That's why I think you're special. I do see God's love in you, Carrie. Just can't figure it all out, I guess," he said.

"Well, let me say one last thing so you can figure it out. On the balloon ride, you told me that all the skills, motivations, wants, and desires of my ancestors were all instilled in me. They didn't know me, yet you say it's supposed to help me. Think about what you said about the Bible." She shut the truck door and walked up the drive towards the house. Uncle Wit put his truck in gear and waved as he left. *Let him chew on that for a while,* she thought. But, Carrie chewed on it, too. She asked the Lord to help him that night. Her prayer was heartfelt and genuine, and she could not shake the feeling that the Lord had plans for him.

CHAPTER 9

A Small Yellow Box

The pen shook in Carrie's hand as she signed her release papers for the adult daycare. On several occasions, she had questioned Uncle Wit about quitting jobs and moving around, and now she was following his modus operandi. *This will be the second job I quit,* she thought. She refused to feel sympathy for him since, by his admission, he didn't need to be saved from anything, but she was beginning to understand that sometimes circumstances arise which require drastic decisions. It was hard for Carrie to see whether this was adult-like or not. She silently prayed Uncle Wit would not hear of it; fear of a disruption in her witness to him filled her heart. "He'll throw it all out of proportion and use it as an argument against me," she reasoned.

The time was 3:15 on Wednesday, and Kate was beside herself that Carrie would choose to resign and could not understand what had happened, but she asked one last time before she filed the papers in her cabinet.

"Carrie, is there any way we can work this out? We have a few special needs residents that are younger and not a risk like that. But, you should never run out on your fears. Dying is part of living. You are doing so well here," Kate said with a groan.

"I'm so sorry. I don't want to disappoint anyone. I can't take death right now and have no desire to be around it. My parents kill animals for a living, and I will never get used to it. If I stayed, I would begin wondering who's next, and I don't want to go to bed thinking about that. You've been so nice to me, and I know I'm not being very adult-like, but this is one thing I have to do for myself," Carrie said.

"Did you open the box, Carrie?" Kate asked. "Does this have something to do with that?"

"You told me I shouldn't talk about it," Carrie replied.

"Now, Carrie, don't be like that. You can tell me what was in it, can't you?" Kate questioned.

"I was so upset the other night, I forgot. I think it's in my smock's pocket. I'll look when I get home," she said.

"Carrie! You must find it!" Kate surprised herself with the quick retort and then quickly lowered her tone and volume. "I mean, you just must. It's something very special, I'm sure—" Kate was interrupted.

"Do you know something about that box, Kate?" Carrie anxiously asked. "You're acting kind of peculiar."

"Oh, Carrie, just find it for me, will you?" Kate said.

"Kate, tell me what you know before I leave. . .please tell me. What is it?" Carrie pleaded.

"I don't really know, but Edd winked at me in a mysterious way when he handed that to me. He made me promise to give it to you someday. . .but. . .then. . .he said something I will never forget. He said, 'Most of us go through life not expecting much, only what we can do for ourselves. Isn't it great when the unexpected happens?' Then, he went and waited for you in the commons. He sat for an hour looking out the window. He watched you pull up, never took his eyes off of you. Carrie, he was so happy to see you. He loved you like his own child," Kate said.

Carrie began to cry and sat down in the side chair. It was too much, too soon. Kate had already been here once before with her and purposely didn't try to hand her a tissue. She sobbed again as she tried to speak. Kate could not understand what she was trying to say but made out a few words about trusting God.

"Carrie, go home now and find the box. You owe it to yourself. We'll discuss it later. Call me if you need to talk," Kate said as she helped lift her from the chair with both hands and led her to the door.

"Okay, Kate, I'll see you another time. I'm sorry," Carrie cried broken heartedly.

"The funeral is tomorrow at Crescent Cemetery, in Crescent just north of here. It's at two o'clock if you want to ride with me," Kate said.

"I'll call you if I decide to, Kate. Thanks for everything," Carrie said.

Carrie left the daycare center without looking back. She had parked her car in a manner that allowed her to leave straight out of the parking lot. She felt relieved and heartbroken at the same time. She punished herself with negative thoughts about being so naïve with the ramifications of working with the elderly. "Why didn't I see that coming?" she asked herself. "I must stop and think these things through. My mother was right. I'm having trouble with the thinking things through concept," she said aloud.

Carrie arrived home to find her mother on the phone. Carla didn't see her come in as she had her back to the kitchen door that serviced the garage. Carrie stood there long enough to make out that the conversation was with Uncle Wit. Her mother seemed irritated with him, but not in the way that she usually talked to him. It was a disagreement about unfinished tasks of sort, not at all callous or cruel.

Carrie revealed her presence and shut the door hard enough to bait a response. Carla said a quick goodbye and hung up the phone. "Oh, I didn't hear you drive up, Carrie; you scared me," she said.

"Yeah, Mom, you scared me, too," Carrie said as she walked past her and up the stairs.

"What does that mean?" her mother called out. "Carrie. . .Carrie, what are you doing home?"

There was no answer but the sound of a closing door. After a short time, Carrie's mother quietly walked up the stairs to Carrie's bedroom. With the door closed, she stood in the hallway and eavesdropped on a discussion with Zeb about the end to her job. Fortuitously, Carrie had placed Zeb on speaker phone while she changed her clothes, and Carla heard both sides of the conversation. Carrie was headed to Zeb's house to use the computer for the ancestral research. "Zeb, can you believe my mother was right? I just need to think things through," Carrie said. The comment elicited a mild smile across Carla's face, and she dropped her head as she prayed a quick prayer of thanksgiving.

Suddenly, loud thumps sounded behind Carla as Pete bounded up the stairs. "Mom, what are you doing?" Pete asked.

"Just coming to get your dirty clothes and some hangers, Pete. Go get your empty hangers for me," she said.

Carrie cracked the door open with a shirt held in front of her. "Mom, what are you doing?" Carrie asked as her mother was rounding the corner into the bathroom.

"Just getting the dirty clothes, honey," she called back.

Carrie shut the door, quickly dressed, and looked out into the hallway again.

"Mom? You still up here?" she called out. Carrie was feeling the need to speak about Uncle Wit and his appearance in the ice cream shop, but as her mother came from the bathroom, the nursing smock caught her eye. Bound up in the dirty laundry from the bathroom hamper, her smock found its way into her mother's armload. "Um, Mom, wait a minute," she said.

Carrie searched the pockets. Then she reached into one and grabbed the brown paper wrapped box. *That was immature of me,* Carrie thought. She wondered what might have happened if her mother had found it, and she sighed in relief.

Carla gave no mind to the find but asked, "Carrie, have you decided what you're wearing to the prom? It's in two and half weeks, ya know?" her mother asked.

"Oh, Mom, I forgot. I mean the girls at school talk about it, but April just seemed so far away. What's the date today?" Carrie asked.

"It's March eighteenth. Haven't you looked at dresses yet?" her mother asked.

"Mom, my job was keeping my brain so busy, and my homework is backed up. . .oh, I don't even have a date," she fretted.

"Well, honey, there's still time. I didn't have a date to my prom until one night before, but I had my dress ready, even if I had to go alone. Steven Yardley finally asked me on the phone," she said with a laugh.

"Nobody will ask me to the prom, Mom; they still call me No-No," she said.

"Call Zeb," her mother suggested.

"Are you kidding me? He's almost twenty. Can I bring somebody out of school, anyway?" Carrie asked.

"Yes, you can. I found out. . .well, not because of you. The school emailed a video to the parents. I would have assumed you watched it, too, Carrie," her mother said.

"My job had control of my time, Mom. I'm out of it. But, I'm free now because. . .well. . .I quit my job, Mom."

Carrie didn't want her mother to see her cry as she had tears forming. She turned her head and walked slowly down the hall to her room with her gift from Edd cupped in her hands. She hoped her mother would chase after and wrap loving arms around her. Carrie made it to her room and shut the door. Mother didn't call out, didn't run after her, and didn't knock at the door. And Carrie was alone with a little brown paper wrapped box.

In her dresser mirror, she saw the face of another girl framed in a wooden white oval looking at her precious brown box. She pretended to be jealous of her reflection and gripped the box tightly. "I think it's time," she said aloud.

Carrie's hands shook as she unwrapped the brown paper carefully, imagining Edd folding each corner as she did. Under the brown paper was a small yellow box with the lid taped. She shook the box for a hint, but still there was little sound. Carrie slid the edge of her nail file under the lid and sliced through a barrier of tape. Carefully and reverently she removed the lid. There, nestled tightly in packed cotton was a funny shaped object that looked very familiar, yet this particular one was foreign to her. The object was shiny and smooth, and she could make out symbols stamped into it. As she placed the lid on the dresser, she saw writing on the inside of it. It was a note from Edd.

Carrie,

I can't tell you how much your friendship has meant to me, so I'll show you. I want you to use this gift for success. You deserve it. My children do not need it. They are well taken care of, so do not feel guilty. It's yours. I'm so proud of you, as if you were one of my own.

Love, Edd

Carrie remembered Kate's words as she described what Edd said. She wondered what it was that was so unexpected. She looked at the gift again but was interrupted by a knock on the door. She quickly replaced the lid and put it in a drawer.

When Carrie opened the door, her mother stood with opened arms and wrapped them around her. She accepted the thoughtfulness due to her wishful feelings earlier, but now, intrigue had filled her mind, and her thoughts were on the small gift. She managed to offer up the reason for her quick departure earlier not realizing her mother already knew.

"Mom, I lost my favorite client on Monday, Edd. He had a heart attack. I was very upset about it," she said while still embracing her mother.

Her mother gently pushed her away to look into her eyes. "Why did you feel the need to quit?" she asked.

"You and dad euthanize animals every week. I don't like your job; you know that. I don't like all the death. If I stayed at the daycare center, all I would wonder is who's next. I can't do it, Mom. I should have seen it coming, I guess," Carrie said.

"You should never worry about death, Carrie. Worry about life and how you want to live. There's plenty to worry about. Worry about Uncle Wit," she said, trying to get a laugh.

"I wish you wouldn't have mentioned him, Mom. Sit down here. I want to ask you something." Carrie's voice changed, and her mother noticed with a cocked head and a funny look.

"Okay," she agreed.

"I'm just going to ask you straight out, and I want you to be honest with me. I know that you've been going around behind my back, but I don't know why," Carrie said.

"Carrie, what is it? I'm not sure I know where you're going with this, but if you're going to ask, then just do it," her mother said.

"Okay, I will. Why did you send Uncle Wit to spy on me at the ice cream parlor when I apologized to Mr. Gibson?" Carrie asked.

"Carrie, I didn't ask him to do that. What put that notion in your head?" Carla said.

"Uncle Wit told me you did!" Carrie snapped back.

"Now, Carrie, I came in here to ease your mind and talk with you about your troubles. I never thought I would be accused of espionage," her mother protested.

"Well, how did Uncle Wit know I was going to go there in the first place?" Carrie asked.

"I told him you were going to set things right with Mr. Gibson. Zeb mentioned it to me at church Sunday after the service. It was just in passing, promise, no secret agent stuff, Carrie," her mother said in jest. "But that explains Wit's phone call. I wondered where he had seen you," her mother mumbled.

An awkward silence came over Carrie. Her mother stared at her. Carrie looked away. She had taken herself out of the situation emotionally and wanted to see what came next in the life-reel she was creating. She waited until her mother made the first move.

"Carrie, look at me. I told your Uncle Wit because he called me the other day, out of the blue on Sunday night. He wanted to apologize for the balloon ride incident. It was a strange phone call. He has never done that before. It was awkward. I tried to be pleasant, and since we were on the topic of apologies, I mentioned your plans with Mr. Gibson. But, Carrie, I did not tell him to go over there. You'll just have to believe me. Come to think about it, he's called four or five times since the balloon ride. I know he called the day of your interviews a few months back, because he wanted to talk to you that day," her mother said.

"Mom, I heard you on the phone with him today when I came in, and you sounded a bit upset with him."

"Carrie, I was. . .a little. He called again today, and I was trying to understand him and his point of view, but now. . .don't get your feelings hurt, sweetheart, but he wants you to stop witnessing to him. He wanted me to talk to you," her mother said.

"Wow, I'm actually bugging him now," Carrie said, laughing.

"It looks like it; I told him he could deal with that on his own. I think he's feeling the hand of the Lord on his life, Carrie. Just be careful," her mother said. "Oh, and by the way, what road trip did you take with him? He mentioned going to Nebraska, over the river into Omaha?"

"Oh, I helped him deliver a package, Mom, but he called you the other day to apologize, then today to stop me from witnessing to him? I wonder why he came to the ice cream parlor in the first place?" she said.

"He loves you, Carrie, but sometimes I wonder if he likes to see people fail," her mother said.

Carrie suddenly pictured a lightbulb above her head like in the cartoon strips. It was not flashing but glowing brightly—with a rainbow of colors pouring out like a waterfall. It made so much sense to her.

"No, Mom. . .I think I got it. He's reaching out, and he doesn't even know it. He wants our interaction; there's no other way to explain it. He wanted to see how an apology worked. Then he got cold feet after I pushed him a little," Carrie said. "Mom, he's going to make the most difficult decision of his life, and he won't regret it. I got this. Wow, that pastor really had it right, and you, too, Mom. The Lord works in mysterious ways."

CHAPTER 10

Ancestral Knowledge

Carrie left the house with a revitalized spirit, rehearsing many different scenarios in her head concerning Uncle Wit. She wanted to be prepared for anything, and any conversation-ditching he had up his sleeve. *I do my best wordwork in the car. Time for another road trip with Uncle Wit,* she thought. But it would have to wait because she promised Zeb an ear about the ancestral search.

Arriving late, Zeb was sitting on the porch steps waiting for her, but had his laptop sitting on the concrete stoop. "There you are, I thought you forgot. Let's go inside. I have to show you this," he said.

Apparently, Zeb had been working on a search for weeks. Notes of every kind were strewn across his mother's sewing table, which was now a computer research center. There were clipboards with labels; Military, Census Records, Births, Deaths, Immigration, and Occupation, and many more in the stack. He plugged the power supply to the laptop and gathered chairs for them both.

"I want to show you something I've been working on. I've been working on you," he said.

"Me?" Carrie said.

"Well, I knew you would never do it, so I started it for you hoping you would like what you saw and take it over from here. But, to tell you the truth, I had a lot of fun with it, and I kept working. There are many records that go way back, but they're not necessary for what I want to show you."

"So all this stuff is from a search on my family tree?" she asked.

"No, some is from my family, too, but you will see what I mean"

"Okay, what's so great about my family tree?" she said.

"Let me say this. Your family is amazing; I couldn't believe what I found. The best thing was from the battle of Fort Sumter at the start of the Civil War. Your great grandfather, five or six times back, was a brother to Louis Wigfall, an aid to General Beauregard. Wigfall negotiated the surrender of Fort Sumter after rowing out from the ship to the fort alone. That was brave. I found something else you might like, too. . ."

"Wait, Zeb, how did you find that out?" she asked.

"Well, I just keyed in your parents' names and their parents' names and made links back. Some of them fizzled out, but others had common relatives who are also looking, and they got linked to my search. One person I found was a woman by the name of Bodil Hansen. She's your great, great, great grandmother on your mother's side. Your Mom said she'd heard of her," Zeb said.

"Yes, I have, too," Carrie said. "She came through Ellis Island."

"Yes, but do you know what she did?" Zeb asked.

"No, not really, never thought to ask," Carrie said with a rather impatient exhale.

"You don't sound so interested in this, Carrie. I guess this was a waste of my time. I thought I could really help you with your plans. I get tired of seeing you sad and depressed and moping around. Sometimes I think you just do it for attention. I wish you would just pretend to be interested," Zeb said disappointedly. "There's so much here I really want you to see. These are the people from which you came, Carrie."

It was a real knock on the head for Carrie. For a moment she considered that was the case. Did she want attention, especially attention from him? Carrie tried to put it out of her head and looked around at the data on the table. She knew Zeb was right, she needed help; she was ready to listen.

"Zeb, I'm so sorry, you're right. I am being selfish. I'm ready, let's look at this stuff.

"Thanks, Carrie. It's about time you said that. I am so excited about this stuff. I'm only trying to help, and I think it will if you'll follow. . .So, Bodil Hansen came over from Norway and her family was one of the first to join the Hull House in Chicago," he began.

"Oh, I know all about the history of that place. It was started by Jane Addams and Ellen Star for women and mothers," Carrie explained.

"But, again, do you know what she did?" Carrie shook her head. "She spent a few years there and then headed to New York and opened up some similar ones in the late 1890s. She helped hundreds of little girls, teens, and women fight poverty and hunger. She bathed them each week, and taught them to read and speak English. That was one smart woman," Zeb said. "You can read an article on her I found in the newspaper of the time."

"Oh, I believe you, Zeb," she said.

"I know you like history, so I made a list of your relatives that you can research if you want. I made it look like roots coming down from your name. The first root breaks into two parts; your dad on the left and your Mom on the right. Then each of those breaks for your Mom's Mom and Dad, and your Dad's Dad and Mom," Zeb said.

Carrie laughed, "I know how the chart works, Zeb, I'm not that goofed up."

"No, you don't. Look at the bottom where there was a divorce, a remarriage, and a death. Those are keyed with different letters and numbers that continue the chart on the page indicated. There are thirteen pages to this chart, Carrie," he corrected. He handed her the notebook and she flipped through it.

"I don't know what to say, Zeb," she said.

Don't say anything; just look at one more relative I found. Look on page three. Down the list a bit you will see John Lancaster. He was from Canada, near New Brunswick. His family tree goes way back to the 1500s to the House of Lancaster in England. I found a note from another researcher, probably one of your distant cousins, who is planning a trip to continue the search on him. John was a brother to your great grandfather five generations back. . .I think. When I followed it through, I found royalty, Carrie," Zeb said excitedly.

Carrie's eyes widened, "My father shared that with me a lot growing up, but all I heard was we came from kings and queens. That's all he knew." Carrie laughed.

"I didn't find any candlestick makers, or bakers in your family, but I did find a very interesting occupation of your great grandfather in St. Louis. Have you ever heard of a chiffonier?" Carrie shook her head with a pondering look on her face. "That's a wig maker." Zeb laughed. "But, most of what I found was a lot of educated people on both sides of the family. You come from well-to-do people—people who could handle themselves pretty well. I don't see how you can come up short with ancestors like that. All your worrying is for the birds. You come from good stock, as they say. That's why you speak so well when you're in a pinch. You come by it naturally," Zeb encouraged.

"I appreciate that, Zeb. Can I have this notebook for later?" she asked.

"Take it, I made it for you," he said.

"You sound like my Uncle Wit. He says I come from tangled roots. I think I'm starting to see what he's talking about; at least the historical part of it," she said.

Carrie had no idea Zeb had spent so much time working on her ancestry, and she was feeling like she owed him something. His discernment in matters of the heart and mind were a gift from God, she never doubted that, but Zeb loved to hear he had made a difference in someone's life. It was a motivation that preserved the desire, and God allowed that for him because he sought the Lord's will in most things. Carrie needed answers to important questions often in her life. Her father was always there, but sometimes it was nice talking to a friend. She wanted to let Zeb know how much she trusted him, and this was a great occasion.

"Okay, Zeb, I'm going to change the subject, now, and I'm gonna show you something."

Carrie took out the yellow box she had received from Edd, opened it and showed its contents to him. He stared at it for a second and picked it out of the cotton nest. A tag was attached which pulled a bit of cotton out with it.

"Carrie, do you know what this is?" Zeb asked.

"Well, a key, I guess," she said. "I didn't know it had a tag on it."

Zeb leaned on the table with both elbows. "It's a safe deposit key from First Bank of Omaha," Zeb said.

"Really, why would he give that to me?" she said. "Zeb, look in the lid there."

He read the words and was speechless for a minute. He looked at her with big eyes. "You've got to go there and see what he gave you," Zeb said.

"If I have to go to Omaha again, well, I know just who to take with me. I'm going to take Uncle Wit, so I can get him in the car. He can't run from me then," she said.

Zeb looked confused at what she was saying, so Carrie explained. "Uncle Wit is dealing with some stuff right now and I've been witnessing to him when I can. I'm gonna get him to take me to Omaha. In the car, I'll have another chance to talk with him."

"Oh. . .I was hoping I could go. . .but I understand. Nothing like being tortured into accepting Christ," he said with a strange look.

"Very funny, my preaching isn't torture," she laughed. "It's. . .compelling."

"Carrie, just make sure you don't damage him. Many people will shut off completely if they feel too pressured. Don't push him away. He loves you very much—don't ruin that. Do you know the rules about witnessing?" he asked.

"I didn't know there were rules," Carrie said.

Zeb didn't wait for her to finish, "Don't brag, nag, lag, or sag. That's it in a nut shell."

Carrie laughed. "WHAT?"

"Well, I read it on Christianity.com the other day. I had never heard it before either, but I did know the general principles about witnessing to others, Carrie," Zeb said.

"What does it mean?" she asked.

"Okay, it's like this. Brag simply means not being self-righteous around others. Let your light shine from within, don't force it. Nag refers to how you witness. Don't bother someone about a sin over and over. They'll step closer to Christ by the example you set, not by pushiness. When you lag, you're not showing Christ's example of a hard worker, it's having the diligence in your job and things you do. People are watching. The sag refers to how you present yourself to people. Carrie, nobody wants what you have if it's sad and burdensome. Be happy and willing. It's all in the article on Christianity.com. Go home and read it before you find yourself alone with Uncle Wit, okay? Promise me you will, Carrie," Zeb said.

"Oh, no, Zeb, I don't know if I can witness to him now. Not after that. I've already bragged, and I've nagged for sure. If it's the job thing, then I've lagged, too, but he only knows about one of those. Wow, and sagging has really been something I've done all year. . .at times," she said.

"Carrie, I'm talking about people who constantly do these behaviors. You haven't been around him long enough to make him too scared, but you could. Just be careful," Zeb cautioned. "And, I need to know what's in the bank box, so don't forget to call and tell me."

"Go with me, Zeb. We could tag team him," Carrie quickly said half-jokingly.

"Oh, no. That would really push your uncle away. Can you imagine how he would feel with two people witnessing? Even if I didn't say anything, he would still feel cornered. He would know it was a ploy. You're going alone on this one, but I'll pray about it," Zeb said.

"I know. I'll be careful and thoughtful. . .and easy," Carrie said.

CHAPTER 11

Beautifully Blue

Carrie attended school Thursday and Friday with so many things on her mind. She had promised herself to concentrate on her schoolwork for the last weeks, but it was almost impossible with prom hanging over her head, her need to see the bank, and Uncle Wit's salvation message repeating itself in her head. She was not herself, and the girls at school noticed the daydreaming during lunch.

"Carrie, are you gonna eat that?" Beth asked her. "Carrie? You in there—Earth to Carrie." A couple of girls laughed.

"I'm sorry. What? I mean, no. You can have it, Beth," Carried finally said, then added, "Are you going to the prom, Beth?"

"Oh, yeah. I told you yesterday—remember? Dakota Clark asked me," Beth said.

"I do remember. I guess I'm not myself lately because of all the stuff on my mind," Carrie replied.

"Have you been asked?" Beth questioned.

"No, and I probably won't be. They still call me No-No, Beth. You heard it the other day in the drama room, I'm sure. Terrance Nicolson said it over the sound system from the stage," Carrie said.

"Well, I didn't laugh. I told him to apologize to you about that. Did he?" Beth asked.

"No."

"I heard a couple of guys at Merk's diner asking about you. Guess who one of 'em is?" Beth teased as the other girls around the table leaned in.

"I've already heard—Keggy," Carrie said.

"He was one of them, but his cousin, Sam, was there, too. He is a super nice guy. He goes to school at a private Christian school in Des Moines. He's nothing like Keggy. They were talking about you a lot. Keggy said some good things about you. He even called you a Jesus freak, and believe it or not, Sam thought that was cool," Beth explained.

Carrie began to laugh, and the other girls began to support her asking him out. Carrie felt embarrassed, but was hopeful it might work out. "I know him. I've even talked with him some at Keggy's birthday party a couple of years ago. I saw him at the state basketball tournament, too. It was last December, I think. What does he look like now?" Carrie asked.

Beth looked at the other girls with great concern, her eyes widened, she paused, and the other girls' smiles left their faces. Eventually, Beth laughed out loud, and then turned to Carrie. "We're just playing with you, Carrie. He really is a nice looking guy." They all laughed. "He wears button down shirts; at least, that's what he had on the couple of times I saw him. He's neatly dressed and doesn't say a lot, but he did ask more about you. I heard him ask Keggy," Beth said.

"I always thought he was cute. I just didn't see him a lot since he lives in Des Moines," Carrie said as the girls pushed on her arms with teasing.

"You should call him, Carrie. He probably doesn't know about our prom, so you gotta inform him, girl," one of the other girls said.

"Okay, okay," Carrie said as she grabbed her books. "Just keep it under your hats, ladies."

Carrie arrived home later Friday evening. She took her supper to her room and laid on her bed staring at the ceiling. She had stopped at Zeb's to share the news about Sam. Zeb's girlfriend was there when she arrived, but Mary happily engaged in the conversation with them. Carrie did not seem bothered by the meeting, and Zeb seemed at ease with the situation as well. Carrie did not stay long, but was able to see the look on Zeb's face when she told him the boy attended a Christian school. "That's what you need, a good guy who loves the Lord, Carrie. Go for it. Ask him to take you to the prom. He won't ask you since he's out of the loop around here. You'll have to do it," Zeb said.

Carrie committed to making the call, but would wait until Saturday afternoon to see if the timing would work out for a meeting with the gang Saturday night. She spent the rest of the night in her room talking to Beth on her cell phone, and Beth assured her Sam would accept. Carrie supposed a preemptive call had already been made, but she did not mind.

Carrie woke up early Saturday morning to the sound of her brother Pete laughing at cartoons. He was right below her in the living room, and his high pitched laughter permitted no further slumber. Sam and Uncle Wit immediately came to mind. "First things first," she said as she jumped out of bed feeling thankful for her noisy little brother.

The plans she had for her uncle took precedence over her prom date for the moment. She would call Sam later. Uncle Wit was working at a job that he wanted to keep. She did not want him calling in sick on her behalf. She also needed to know when the bank was open for walk-in business. She turned her computer on and looked up the name printed on the tag of the safe deposit key. Unfortunately, the bank was closed until Wednesday due to remodeling, but extended hours would be in place for the rest of the week. *I can get out of school, pick up Uncle Wit, and still have time to get to the bank,* she thought. She set her mind to getting Uncle Wit in her car, not just for sharing Christ, but to solicit his help with the bank key. She wanted to help him feel needed, a lesson learned from Zeb, and she knew it would go a long way in witnessing Christ. There would be no "brag" on Wednesday. Uncle Wit would be there for her, and she would use that to her advantage.

Carrie grabbed a couple of pieces of paper from her desk drawer. She wrote across the top of one, Uncle Wit, and on the other, Sam Lane. For an hour, Carrie planned her conversations with each. She switched between the two when a thought came to her. She was in her element. She knew she had a gift of gab, but this time, she felt more secure writing down the words for a conversation that could have a long lasting impact on them—and her. In her mind, she knew she was making adult decisions. Never before had she stopped to think about the ramifications of her speech in this way. The past urgings of her mother, father, and others, had finally broken through. She was thinking things through.

"I'm thinking things through!" she said aloud. She laughed and shook her head back and forth. "Mom would never believe it."

Her plans for Uncle Wit would have to wait until Wednesday; the clock in the living room chimed 10:30. It startled Carrie as she was sitting almost asleep in the chair next to it. By now, Carrie had eaten breakfast with her family, cleaned the dishes, readied herself for the day, and was waiting to call Sam Lane. One task was necessary before the call could be made—she wanted her parents' blessing. With confidence, Carrie shook off her fatigue and stood up.

"Mom, I found a date for the prom," she said.

"You did?" her mother said with excitement. "Who is it?"

"Well, do you remember that goofy guy who broke your lamp post outside a couple of years ago?" Carrie asked.

"Oh, him. I hope he's grown up some, Carrie," her mother said.

"No, he hasn't, but it's not him. It's his cousin. His name is Sam Lane," Carrie said.

"When did he ask you, Carrie? What did he say?" her mother asked like a giddy teenager.

"Well—he didn't ask me, Mom. I have to ask him," Carrie said with caution.

"Oh, I see," her mother said as she sat down next to her father on the couch.

Her father looked at Carrie from behind his medical magazine. He slowly placed it on his lap and took over for his wife. Carrie saw the difficulty coming, but could not have assumed it would be her father who would take the lead. Her mother knew Carrie's father wanted to speak, and she, too, wondered what he would say about prom.

"So tell us, Carrie, how did you come to this decision?" her father said.

Carrie sat down. "I really forgot about the prom with all that was going on with my job, and I don't have a lot of time to wait around, Dad," Carrie said.

"I'm sure you've talked about this at school. Are there not boys willing to ask you out there?" he said.

"Dad, they're still calling me No-No at school." She wrinkled her lips to one side of her face. "The answer is, no," she said.

"Well, that doesn't sound good. Are you upset about that, sweetheart?" he asked.

"No. I earned it for sticking up for people—and myself. I don't like it, but I know I earned it on principle, so I'm good," she said.

"Carrie, I'm sure you know that what we say often becomes who we are. The Bible tells us that out of the heart the mouth will speak," he said.

"Dad, I got that nickname for standing up for people and standing my ground. I was not inappropriate with my speech. Maybe I butted in to help other kids, but I never told untruths. I don't want to talk about that anyway. I just want you to know that I'm breaking with tradition, a bit, for a good guy who has no idea about our prom here in Council Bluffs. He's from Des Moines," Carrie said.

"How do you know this boy, Sam?" her father asked.

"Well, like I told mom, he's Keggy's cousin," she said.

"Isn't he the one who broke our lamp post outside?" her father asked.

Pete stood up from his seated position on the floor. He ran to his father and looked in his left ear. Carrie and her mother laughed out loud.

"Check it good, Pete," Carrie said. Her mother laughed again.

"Okay, okay, I get it. So you already said that. My goodness. Go call your Sam before I throw you in the kennel," he said.

Carrie smiled big at her mother, and her mother smiled back. Getting their blessing was a burden lifted. After an hour on the phone, Carrie came down stairs with a smile chiseled into her cheeks. Her mother's face showed relief, and it prompted the presentation of a large box.

"Mom, you didn't?" Carrie yelled.

The box held a beautiful blue, long, V-neck dress, with a floral embroidered bodice and small rhinestones on a thin delicate material. The narrow straps crossed in the back and met the bodice lower than in the front. The bottom was smooth silky satin that would flare out gracefully when she moved. On top of the dress lay a pair of large white, shiny, faux diamond earrings with three teardrops hanging end for end. Carrie took the dress out of the box and held it against her chest. She sashayed to the curio cabinet to look in its mirror while hanging an earring from her right ear. She swirled around her father and brother, but was pushed out of the way of the television by Pete's small hands.

"If you like it, we'll have to get it sized just right, but we don't have a lot of time," her mother said.

"I love it! Thanks, Mom. I love you so much," Carrie said.

"I love you, too, Dear." Her mother smiled.

Carrie came down the stairs after putting on the dress for her mother. She had taken extra time to French braid her hair on the right side. The dress fit perfectly with no alterations needed in Carrie's eyes.

"Oh, my," her mother said, "that is absolutely beautiful. I thought I bought the dress a little big. I just didn't see how much you had grown, Sweetheart. You are perfect and look absolutely beautiful. Old Sam doesn't have any idea what he's in for, does he?" Her mother laughed.

"Carrie, I'm very proud of you," her father said. "I've been sitting here thinking about what you said. You know, my family have always been ones to say what they think. I know you'll make a difference in this world because of that quality. We come from kings and queens, ya know; important people who did make a difference. Our roots go way back to England, and like Uncle Wit likes to say, we all come from tangled roots," he said.

"Dad, he told me that, too," Carrie said.

"Yes, he's said it a lot over the years; especially when you corner him on an issue." He laughed.

"I didn't get it when Uncle Wit said it to me, Dad, because I didn't think he understood it, but now I know what it means. I've thought about it a lot. If my ancestors could make a difference, I can too. Dad, I'm taking it one step further, I'm asking for the Lord's help, so I can make that difference for Him." Carrie stood even prouder in her blue dress.

"Carrie, you are so stately standing there like that. I couldn't be more proud of you." He beamed. He motioned to her to come closer, stood, and hugged her tightly with love and pride. He kissed her cheek and whispered in her ear, "The Lord will guide you when you're in His will."

Carrie smiled at her father and turned to her mother. She saw a large tear running down her mother's cheek as she reached for another hug. The two embraced for short while, and Pete soon joined them.

CHAPTER 12

Miraculous Happenings

Monday and Tuesday were easy days at school. Her mind was free of clutter and issues, and she excelled in her studies. In her History class, she volunteered to debate the latest winner from the state competition on socialism vs. capitalism. Carrie won by some assessments and tied by others. But, she was beginning to feel like herself again, and the worry of growing up was taking a backseat to her anticipation for prom. The girls at school made sure that topic stayed relevant; it was hard to ignore.

Eventually though, Wednesday came, and Carrie's bathroom poster made it clear; the most important decision you will ever have to make. *That's the decision you make with thoughtful considerations of others,* she thought. She had come to understand that life was always better after thinking things through. It was this lesson which she would use with Uncle Wit. She knew they shared some of the same issues;

she was like him in many ways. She knew her mother was right when she said it. She just didn't want to admit it. Uncle Wit's tangled roots were her tangled roots. She thought back to his interaction with the lady at the botanical garden. *He must have a special way of communicating with people,* she thought. *Yep, there's just something about that guy. How did he land all those jobs he's had?*

That was the question she needed. She would get him talking about how he acquired all the jobs. Then, she could work into the conversation any topic she wanted. She could manipulate words like a sculptor manipulated clay. She just needed him to talk.

Wednesday was a normal day, too. Carrie flew from class to class doing her best, interacting with the other students, and impressing the teachers. The last bell rang, and she bolted to her car in the parking lot. She was the first one out of the main gate, even though she received a "Slow Down" gesture from the gate guard. She turned right and headed to Uncle Wit's workplace. She had the small yellow box in the center console.

Unbeknownst to Uncle Wit, Carrie stood by his truck as he returned to go home.

"Carrie, what are you doing here?" he asked surprised.

Carrie mustered up excitement in her voice, "Uncle Wit, I need your help right away. Remember when I told you about the guy who died at my last job? Well, look!" she said as she handed him the yellow box. "He left this to me."

He opened it carefully and stared at it. "This is a bank deposit key. . .have you been to this bank to see what's in the box?" he asked.

"No, Uncle Wit, I don't know how to do it, and I need your help," she said with compassion. "I didn't want anyone but you going with me because I knew you would keep my secret. I wanted to share it with my parents but decided to wait until I find out what's in it. The lady at work gave it to me, and she's wanting to know what I got from him, too," she said. "But I'm afraid of what might be there."

"Carrie, I think you should call your mother and have her go with you; she might be upset if she learns about this," he said.

"You have got to be kidding me!" Carrie said with disappointment. She felt he owed her for the time she took him to Omaha to keep his job. She thought about how he played her after the balloon ride and how he had teased her for years with smart-Alec remarks. Then it dawned on her; he, too, was thinking things through. *Could it be,* she thought, *that I have influenced him that much?* She sat down on the parking block next to the truck. She was angry and at a loss for words. *Uncle Wit wins again,* she thought.

"Carrie, you alright?" he asked.

"No, I'm not. We have been through a lot together in the past years. I've never, wholeheartedly, taken my mother's side in arguments against you. I still talked to you after the hurtful things you did to me, and now, after you shared your secret with me, I wanted to share a secret with you," Carrie said.

Suddenly, a heavy feeling of guilt came over Carrie. The honesty was not there, and he could see right through her. The secret she had was at a cost on his behalf—listening to a salvation message as a captive audience. She did not want to witness to him on those grounds after the lesson from Zeb. She knew she was wrong, and it would be outside of the will of God to hide her true intentions.

"Uncle Wit, you're a smart man. Do you know what I had in mind for you today?" she asked.

"Yes, I do. You wanted to preach to me again, I'm sure," he said with a laugh.

"That's right, I did, but I still need your help with this safe deposit key thing. Will you please go with me? I promise no preaching if you do, but I do want to ask you some questions, if I can?" she asked.

"I knew you had something up your sleeve, because I knew Zeb would have been your best choice if you wanted a secret kept. It was very obvious. Did your mother tell you I called?" he asked.

"Yes, and that hurt my feelings, Uncle Wit," she scolded.

"I'm sorry, Carrie. I had a lot of things on my plate, but I've been listening to you. I keep tabs on you, too. You're a good example, even for an old guy like me. I was really impressed about you givin' that money to Mr. Gibson at the ice cream shop. It showed me who you really are. I've been thinking about what you said to me on the balloon ride, too. You were right about that; I never did seek the Lord's direction for my live. I want you to know that I'm trying, and it's because of what you said to me," he responded.

"What did I say?" Carrie asked.

"You said you were always taught to trust the Lord for things you needed, and that my approach was worldly; that's why I felt like I was drifting around. That spoke to me, Carrie. Oh, I was a little upset, but I haven't forgotten it, and I don't want to hear anymore preaching, that's for sure. I can watch and learn a lot from you, Carrie. I'm old enough to admit I can still learn," he said.

"Okay, deal. But, will you please go with me to the bank? I'm truly scared about what's in that box," Carrie said.

"Alright, I'll do it. Let's go, kiddo. But, I don't think you need to be afraid of a gift," he said.

Uncle Wit moved to jump in his truck, but Carrie jumped in her car. She sat and motioned for him to get in. He rolled his eyes at her, took his keys out of the ignition, and locked his truck. "No funny stuff, now." He laughed as he got in her car.

The ride over the river to Omaha was longer than usual due to five o'clock traffic. They talked about the past times and how her mother had always had it out for him. Carrie got him to admit he was hard on her, and he seemed to have some remorse for it. She shared her feeling towards him at times and explained the animosity that had grown between her and her mother. Uncle Wit surprised her with an important thought, "Other things may change us, but we start and end with the family."

"Who said that; where did you hear it?" Carrie asked.

"It was on the wall at the Red Cross. It took me several minutes to work out what it said." He laughed. "Anthony Brandt said it."

"Well, who is he?" Carrie asked.

"I don't know; it was just on a poster in one of those rooms. He must be a musician since there were music notes all over the poster," he said. They were helping me with some things a while ago. I remembered it because it reminds me of you and of all my family. It's true though, Carrie."

Carrie could not believe her ears. Even posters were common between them; and meaningful ones, no less. "My favorite poster says this, 'The most important decision you will ever have to make.' It reminds me to be adult-like and think things through," she said.

"What bank are we going to? I think that's it." He pointed.

Carrie felt nervous, like the day of the balloon ride. She parked the car in the bank's parking lot and they walked in. An astute woman met them at the front, questioned them as to their need, then led them to a private room with a curtain and closed it behind her as she left.

Uncle Wit looked at the key, "Let's see, 170, section two," he mumbled. "There it is, Carrie, that's your box," Uncle Wit said.

"What do you think is in it? Edd said his kids didn't need it, whatever it is. What don't kids need from their own father?" Carrie asked.

The room wasn't dark, but the ceiling was painted black with pin lights and spotlights embedded in it. The floor, too, was black, but it was covered with a plush carpet. The lights shined down on things below like in a finely lit museum. There was a special warm ambiance to the room.

"Oh, Carrie, just open it and see," Uncle Wit said anxiously.

Carrie's hand shook as she carefully took the key from its cotton nest in the yellow box. She placed the key in the lock. She turned it, and a long drawer-like box was released. She pulled it.

"Take it all the way out, Carrie, and bring it over to the table," Uncle Wit said.

She did as he asked, and laid it on a black velvet cloth draped across the table. The lid was hinged in the far back of the box. She lifted the long awkward lid all the way back, and Uncle Wit held it up. Inside was a small child's shoebox from years ago, and another more recent box. Carrie took the newer box out and placed it on the table. Wrapped around the box was old style tying twine, and Uncle Wit cut it with his pocket knife along with the string on the other box. As Carrie opened the cardboard box, a white envelope glowed from the lights overhead. Surprised to see her name on it, her hands began shaking. Uncle Wit reached over to help steady her hand.

"Read it out loud, please," he said.

Carrie,

Please accept this gift from me. You have been a great friend these past months. As you know by now, I am rather wealthy. My children will be taken care of very nicely. I wanted you to have my rainy day fund I've been adding to for years. I never got to use it. I have never needed it, so I want you to have it. You can use it to get your life started one day, not that you can't on your own. I know the Lord has so many plans for you. Your gift will help so many. Carrie, you are one who cares about people. Most of us go through life not expecting much, only what we can do for ourselves. Isn't it great when the unexpected happens?

Your Friend,
Edd Gilbert

Under the envelope sat four bundles of paper money.

"Wow! Carrie, that was nice," Uncle Wit exclaimed.

"I—I—I can't believe it," Carrie stammered.

"Carrie, some of those are hundreds!" Uncle Wit said loudly.

"Keep your voice down," Carrie said.

Carrie lifted one of the stacks and counted the bills. It took some time, but she finally stated that it was close to $10,000. There were three more similar stacks in the box. Uncle Wit put his hands to his face in disbelief.

"Who does this?" he said picking up the small child's shoebox from the drawer. "Look at the dates in this box. These are bills from the 1950s, and some are Silver Certificates. These are collector's items. Some of these are worth more than the face value. Wow, some of these are old," he said excitedly.

"These aren't old. Look, this one says 2012, and this one is 2018," Carrie said.

"You have the last bills he added. This Edd guy added money to these boxes his whole life. Look at this old box, it's probably from his little girl's shoes years ago. Probably when he first married. He must have put money in this box every time he got paid," Uncle Wit said.

"Should we leave the money here for safe keeping?" Carrie asked.

"Edd probably rented this safe deposit box recently just for you. It's a good thing you didn't wait any longer than you did. Since he's dead and nobody else is on the account they could close it out. I'm just not sure about it. We better take it and leave the key with that lady. I'll get her and explain. We better put the money in the boxes, Carrie. Nobody needs to see what we carry out of here," Uncle Wit stated.

Uncle Wit was gone for a short while, which left Carrie alone for a moment. She stared at the money, and said a short prayer of thanks to God. Her parents would be beside themselves. She thought of ways she could thank them using it, but she reconsidered when she realized that the Lord was dealing with her just as much as she had hoped He was dealing with Uncle Wit. It was a life-changing moment of clarity for her.

Carrie stood still and stared again at the walls in the safe room. Hundreds of little boxes lined three walls of the room, and she wondered what each might hold. She wondered if they held money, jewels, secrets, precious other things all locked up tightly and safely hidden away, or did they hide things meant never to be seen? She wanted to open each one—to look inside—not to take—just to know. She wondered what it would be like to have a master key; a key that could open every box. She looked at the key in her hand and thanked God, again, that it opened one box for her. Suddenly, tears formed in her eyes. "I can't believe what is happening to me," she said aloud quietly. She looked at the crimson curtain separating her from the world. Unexpectedly, chill bumps spilled down her back and arms, her head tilted back, and her face was confronting a bright spot light embedded in the ceiling. She saw the words scroll through the light like a marquee at a theater, "THE MOST IMPORTANT DECISION YOU WILL EVER HAVE TO MAKE." The sight frightened her as the vision appeared so real. She reached out toward the table to steady herself; she was dizzy and disoriented. She felt enabled in a way she had never felt before. Her ears were ringing, and tears from both eyes joined under her chin and dropped unto one of the shoe boxes. She understood. She swallowed hard and accepted with a perceptible nod what the Lord had just shown her.

Uncle Wit came back through the curtain and started to speak, but Carrie wrapped her arms around him and happily said with a tearful tone, "I know what to do now! It's been there in front of my face the whole time! I have a gift, the money to see it through, and friends and family who will support me the whole way. And, I have the master key to it all," she said.

There was a pause, as if Carrie thought Uncle Wit knew what she was talking about.

"Well, what is it, Carrie?" he said with concern for the tears in her eyes.

"I'm going into the ministry!" she yelled a bit louder than she should have for being in a bank.

"Preacher?" Uncle Wit said astounded.

"Yes, preacher, minister, pastor, whatever you want to call it, I'm okay with it. But, there's a lot of different forms of ministry," she said. "I'm going to research it tonight. Too many things have happened to me to let this go. The Lord's dealing with me, Uncle Wit. Me!" Carrie exclaimed.

The woman came through the curtain and quietly placed the metal box back into the opening. She thanked them and handed Carrie a thick, black, plastic bag for her boxes. Carrie gave the woman the key, and she and Uncle Wit returned to the car.

Carrie was still reeling with excitement from the ordeal in the bank safe room. Uncle Wit was quiet, and she presumed he was avoiding an obligatory end to the agreement about witnessing. He looked out the window to the right as they traveled toward Council Bluffs. She knew she did not have to say a word. He knew. He saw. He could not deny the hand of God on her life. If he wanted to watch her like he said, she expected he would go cross-eyed doing it.

The ride was interrupted by a strange sounding beeping noise coming from under the dash of the car. The gas gage light was flashing red, and the hand showed her tank near empty.

"Whoa, I better get gas before we run out," she said. "I hope I have enough money on me!" she said.

Uncle Wit laughed a hardy laugh with her as she pulled over into a station. It was a beautiful evening and Uncle Wit hinted about getting something to eat.

"I wonder what's around here, Carrie. Anything good?" he said as he helped her with the gas nozzle. She noticed he seemed preoccupied as he looked up and down the street for signs of fast food.

"I'll run in and pay if you want to stay here; I'll let you know when you can pump," she said.

"Carrie do you need the box?" he asked inaudibly.

"No, I'll leave that alone around here," she said. "You never know who's watching."

After a few minutes, Carrie tried to get his attention while inside the store, and she called Uncle Wit's name several times as she walked toward the car, but he did not respond. As Carrie got closer, she could see him shaking slightly, as if he was sick and with chills. He was leaning on the car, and his face was red and warm. She laid her hand on his back.

"Uncle Wit? You sick buddy?" she asked, but he did not answer. Tears welled up in his eyes as she took the gas nozzle out of his hands. Uncle Wit slowly made his way back into the car and sat with his face in his hands. Carrie filled the tank and jumped into the car with concern. She moved the car out of the way of the pumps and stopped along the edge of the property.

"Are you sick, Uncle Wit? What happened?" she asked.

Uncle Wit slowly looked at her and then pointed with his eyes toward the next block. A large sign on twin pillars raised up and out of the clutter of the surroundings. It was a beautiful yellow sign with bright blue letters. Carrie took a minute to read it, then looked at him with amazement. Understanding the reality of the situation, she read it again aloud so Uncle Wit could hear it and understand. "Omaha Word and Fellowship, Pastor Dakota Red Leaf, Sunday worship service 9:00 a.m. and 11:00 a.m., Wednesday night service 6:00 p.m."

A long pause followed; neither wanted to speak. The miracle was obvious. Each realized the gravity of the circumstance and how the Lord was moving. The silence solidified the moment for both of them. Carrie understood the sudden emotional change in Uncle Wit.

"I'm, I'm healed, Carrie," he said with a slight shutter in his voice.

"What?" she asked.

With tears still in his eyes, Uncle Wit took her hand and explained. "Carrie, I read that sign as fast as you did. I've never read that fast before, never. Carrie, I'm healed. I can read. The service starts in ten minutes. I have some things to get off my chest. Will you go with me?" Uncle Wit began to cry again as Carrie patted his knee.

"Oh, will I!" she said with spirit. "Let's go, Uncle Wit."

"I have a lot to clear up with your mother, too; and my parents. It's been a while, but I know I have to do it," he said.

Carrie drove over to the next block and parked the car in front of a large stucco walled building. It seemed newly constructed and welcoming. Pastor Red Leaf stood in the vestibule greeting guests as they arrived. As Uncle Wit entered, he made eye contact with him, despite his tears, and they threw their arms around each other.

"I've been expecting you," Pastor Red Leaf said quietly with emotion.

Uncle Wit regained his composure before the service and apologized to Pastor Red Leaf for his words and behavior on the balloon ride. Carrie and Uncle Wit enjoyed a lovely service, and after the service, Carrie received encouraging words from the pastor and was offered help in her journey into the ministry. The pastor also gave her many leads and a list of credible schools she could explore. Carrie understood the gift of money even more as they talked about educational costs. She knew that her last decision was one that would make a big difference in many lives. She knew she had great help waiting for her at home; there would be no rash decisions, only prayerful and thoughtful resolutions.

During the service, Carrie pondered how her tangled roots had somehow prepared her for this moment. *My ancestors would be proud,* she thought. His "tangled roots" would lead to salvation by God's grace and give him the most exciting chapter in his life yet. It was an absolute wonder in Carrie's eyes, how the Lord could bring everything together as He did. Carrie gained more clarity about her own story each time she shared it with the people in attendance. A nice afterglow meal, as the pastor explained, was served in the dining hall for those who stayed. The attendees in the night's service were supportive of Wit. Healing was a wonderful thing for his life, and accepting Christ was even better. He laughed in a worshipful spirit of thanksgiving for all that had happened as he caught the eye of the woman from the botanical garden.

TODD R. GUNDERSON

Todd is a native of North Dakota, but is currently living in Tennessee. Having lived in each location for approximately twenty-five years, he enjoys the unique perspective and experience of the two completely different cultures. He writes stories that seek and capture the essence of life from both areas. Many of the trials and events he writes about come from personal experiences in his own life. He also loves researching elements of his stories for that added knowledge a reader may glean from the pages. Todd has twenty-five years of teaching experience in grades three–seven and is currently teaching in an elementary school. Todd is also a custom woodworker, and loves building and working with his hands. He is married with four children, one grandchild, two dogs, and two outdoor cats, and they all love the country life. He wishes to write books that are hard for any reader to put down.

www.ingramcontent.com/pod-product-compliance
Lightning Source LLC
Chambersburg PA
CBHW052010240626
47153CB00008B/2821

9781950385454